THE WOLF'S MAGE

Stephanie –
Hope you
love the Enchanted
Rock Immortals
as much
as I do!
Amanda

Be sure to get all of Amanda's exciting stories, available exclusively through Kindle and Kindle Unlimited!

The Enchanted Rock Immortals World

The Puma's Second Chance—FREE!
The Wolf Shifter's Redemption
The Demon's Shifter Mate
The Fae's Obsession
The Shifter's Savior
The Lion Shifter's Trust
The Gargoyle Dilemma
The Demon's Choice
The Fae's Future
Immortal Conspiracy: An Enchanted Rock Immortals Box Set
Immortal Intrigue: An Enchanted Rock Immortals Box Set
Immortal Seduction: An Enchanted Rock Immortals Box Set

The Flannigan Sisters Psychic Mysteries

Finders Keepers
Ghosts, Pies, & Alibis
Murder Most Merry
Fourth and Long
Ghosts, MOs, & a Baking Show
Last Rodeo
Crash and Burn
Gossip, Ghosts, and Grudges
Seasons Slayings

The Enchanted Rock Immortals World
Releases by Author

Eve Cole

Avian
The Dragon's Phoenix
Alpha
Anomaly
The Mate Maker
The Rook's Mate
The Shifter's Assassin
The Shifter's Thief
Avian, Anomaly, The Rook's Mate:
  An Enchanted Rock Immortals Novella M/M Box Set
The Dragon's Phoenix, Alpha, the Mate Maker:
  An Enchanted Rock Immortals Novella M/F Box Set

Fenley Grant

Sorcery, Snakes, and Scorpions: A Love Story
Witches, Werewolves, and War: A Love Story
Unwed, Unfed, and the Undead: A Love Story
Curses, Cats, and Crime: A Love Story
Pinwheels, Potions, and Possibilities: A Love Story
Twists, Turns, and Telekinetics: A Love Story
Aliases, Artifacts, and Attraction: A Love Story
Rings, Rituals, and Rock & Roll: A Love Story
Mistletoe, Merriment, and Murder: A Love Story
Moonlight, Magic, and Mayhem: A Clan Magic Box Set, Vol. 1
Moonlight, Magic, and Mayhem: A Clan Magic Box Set, Vol. 2

Robin Lynn

Of Magic, Love, and Fangs
The Demon King's Runaway Bride

Susan Person

Fae Undone
Fae Redone

Amanda Reid

The Puma's Second Chance—FREE!
The Wolf Shifter's Redemption
The Demon's Shifter Mate
The Fae's Obsession
The Shifter's Savior
The Lion Shifter's Trust
The Gargoyle Dilemma
The Demon's Choice
The Fae's Future
The Shifter's Sorcerer
The Wolf's Mage
Immortal Conspiracy: An Enchanted Rock Immortals Box Set
Immortal Intrigue: An Enchanted Rock Immortals Box Set
Immortal Seduction: An Enchanted Rock Immortals Box Set

Sharla Wylde

A Mermaid's Choice—FREE!
A Mermaid's Quest
A Merman's Mission
A Mermaid's Rescue
Atlantis Revealed: An Enchanted Rock Immortals Box Set

All titles available exclusively in Kindle and Kindle Unlimited!

THE WOLF'S MAGE

AN ENCHANTED ROCK IMMORTALS NOVELLA

AMANDA REID

ISBN 978-1-951770-19-8

Demons and Vampires. Elves and Fairies. Mages and Witches. Werewolves and Dragons. Psychics and Telekinetics.

These magical beings and more exist, rubbing shoulders in their daily lives with unsuspecting humans. But a supernatural society doesn't happen without order. Millennia ago, the Clans —Sanguis, Fae, Magic, Shifter, and Human Paranormal— wisely formed a Council to maintain that order. The end? To ensure the worlds of human and paranormal beings didn't collide and break out into a war that would result in the extermination or subjugation of either.

As human civilization progressed, the first council formed the All Clan Charter at the natural vortex in Great Zimbabwe, giving each clan a voice in the administration of affairs both between the clans and with humans. Next, Asia formed its council at Chengtu Vortex. Then European at Warel Chakra Vortex. North America came next at the natural vortex humans called Enchanted Rock, in what today is known as Texas.

Now, thriving communities of paranormal beings exist in and around the granite outcropping. Humans scrabble over the dome, not suspecting an entire city exists within its confines: the North American Council and all its departments—Legislative, Administrative, Security, Medical, Vortex Transportation, and Legal, plus restaurants, clan hotels, and shops catering to the paranormal crowds.

Also under that dome? Intrigue, politics, and most importantly, love.

These are the stories of The Enchanted Rock Immortals.

1

"I'VE GOT movement on the south side."

Caleb Coffey spoke in a bare murmur, though the vehicle had been spelled so his words wouldn't be heard outside. A click through his ear receiver was the only acknowledgement he received from Mouse, his team member on this surveillance. Further conversation wasn't required until Caleb had garnered more information.

First possible target of the night.

He narrowed his lids to focus all his shifter's enhanced eyesight on the gloom shrouding the derelict building in Elgin, Texas. The shadow was bigger than the rats he'd seen along the adjacent railroad tracks.

Cheese, the Hebert Security analyst, had identified this abandoned cotton warehouse as an Underground crime syndicate holding facility and the possible location for the telekinetic his agency had been hired to find. From where he'd positioned his older-model SUV, he once more studied the two sides of the rusted, corrugated-metal-clad exterior. He should be virtually invisible in the auto repair shop's overnight parking some one hundred yards away. Regardless, he slouched a little further to hide his height by blending with the headrest.

Damn the Underground. The vicious organization had been responsible for the most atrocities since the North American Council Security ended the Pure Paranormal Campaign's ethnic cleansing purges some five years ago. This new organization, however, didn't care if the being was a mixed-blood human paranormal or from Clan Shifter, Fae, Sanguis, or Magic, for that matter. All they wanted was a female because they were "lesser" beings, and all they cared about was how much the paranormal abilities would bring at a black-market auction.

The shadow moved once more, a mere lift of what might be...an arm.

He froze. There. Caleb tamped down on the strange feeling of anticipation. He'd been a security operative for too long to ignore the tickle in his chest indicating something was about to happen. What? He couldn't tell.

"More movement." He didn't need to press a switch as the comms device at his neck activated when he spoke. "Doesn't look like a patrol. Too furtive."

"Multiple?" Mouse's rumbly mumble came through Caleb's communications earpiece from a location on the other side of the derelict structure.

"One at this point." Though he brought his lids to a near squint, he couldn't find the shadow he'd identified moments ago. Anticipation balled in his gut. He slipped on his backpack and prepared to move. "Can't tell what though. Definitely not an animal. Maybe an invisibility spell or some sort of magic shroud."

"Sounds like magic or fae, though if it's a shroud, then it could be anyone."

"Right. Stay alert." If only his boss, Nathan Hebert, stuck with cases within his own clan. But then the alpha of the New Orleans pack was an overachiever. Plus, shifters often used charms and potions bought from Clan Magic or magical items bought or stolen from Clan Fae. Long ago, the clans were more xenophobic, but in today's world, not only did individuals use what they needed from other paranormal beings, they even found mates outside their clan, like several of the wolves in Hebert Security.

Caleb zeroed in on a gloomier shadow. His instinct, more animal than logical, said the being was there.

"Found it again. Still no sign—"

The streetlights extinguished at the same time dark figures swooped down from above.

His heart rate kicked up. "Gargoyles. At least three." Sparks and spells started flying toward the fae beings. "They're on the shadow, probably mage or sorcerer."

"Should we assist?"

Dammit. This was supposed to be a surveillance only mission and one of three in the central Texas area. The closest other team was in northern Austin, over twenty miles away. "I don't think we can wait for the rest of the crew. We're going to lose any victims here anyway when the assholes realize they've been discovered. No use one more victim dying or getting captured. Maybe we can save a few before they transfer them."

"Meet you on the south side."

Caleb exited and shut the door behind him, hoping to not draw the gargoyles' attention with his movement. The night's strong winds would hinder both sound and scent. Nonetheless, he kept his hearing sharp for a wing's flap, since there may be more on patrol overhead. The bastards were tough with their stony hides, claws, and strength. Though he hated to admit it, they were usually tougher than the shifters the fae bred them from.

Racing toward the fight, he pulled the gun from the holster he wore at the small of his back and thumbed off the safety. With a gargoyle's nearly impenetrable skin, the spelled bullets would work faster than he could with his own fae knife. Luckily, his boss also paid for sound-deadening rounds. Regular humans, people who were largely unaware of the paranormal world that existed right under their noses, would react to gunshots and complicate the matter. Though, he probably didn't need to worry about the sound with the bright fireworks slung by the magic-wielder.

He dashed across the potholed, macadam-paved side street, then over the twin set of railroad tracks, gaze glued to where the magic-wielder had been pressed back into a corner. The fight would be over soon if no help arrived.

Since shifters were four times as strong as a human but only half as strong as a gargoyle, he aimed and fired at one of the granite-skinned fae who'd moved far enough away that Caleb would chance the headshot. The opponent dropped as if his life were attached to an on/off switch.

Caleb felt zero remorse. The injury wouldn't kill him, but it would ruin this male's next week.

Whoever lobbed the spells must still be cloaked, since all he could discern were shadows. Didn't matter. He pressed forward.

A wing's whisper caused him to pivot and fire. He caught a descending opponent in the chest, then added another in the head while the gargoyle fell like lead from the sky.

When he turned back, Mouse had joined the fray. Not many knew the other wolf shifter had gargoyle in his genetic history.

He didn't need a gun since his strength easily matched his opponent's. Mouse clocked one of the stony fae in the face and sent the body flailing wings over ass into the air.

The fae landed at Caleb's feet, and he promptly placed another spelled round squarely in the back of the gargoyle's head. Easy enough.

Two opponents remained, making four guards in total. Mouse kept one occupied, while the magic-wielder fought the other but was losing ground.

Caleb moved to the side to get a clean shot at the same time the fae's stony fist met the cloaked being's jaw.

A double tap on Caleb's trigger ensured the gargoyle wouldn't be getting up any time soon. He shifted his focus to his partner. Mouse landed the shot and dropped his opponent to the ground. Caleb approached and squeezed a headshot for good measure.

"Thanks."

"Welcome," Caleb said. "I'm going to check out the victim—can you bind the granite guys, then call Hebert? I'm guessing he'll want Clan Shifter Security to clean up this mess rather than NACS." With so many beings captured for sale on the black market, even North American Council Security, the entity that policed the continent's paranormal community, had taken notice of the Underground. But with NACS came more government red tape. His own clan's security would be easier to work with since he knew many from his stint there.

"On it." Mouse pulled a set of bindings from where they hung on the side of his backpack.

Caleb moved to the small heap of shadows on the ground, which had begun to stir. He'd learned the hard way that a groggy paranormal could take him as a threat, so he kept a respectful distance. "You okay?"

"Ungh..." A hood had fallen away revealing the back of a head, dark hair pulled into a thick, neat bun. Paired with the breathy gurgle, the style led him to believe the victim was a female. She pushed to all fours, then rose stiffly from the ground.

He didn't blame her—a gargoyle's punch could easily break a jaw, evidenced by her hand, which rose to tentatively probe where the fae landed the blow.

Though he scanned the skies for more attackers, nothing met his sharp gaze. A cautious relief trickled through him, and he returned his focus to the female. "We're friendlies, but we may want to get you under cover."

Her back shot ramrod straight and she turned, her features screwed into a scowl. With seething venom, she said, "I'm not going anywhere until I look inside and see for myself."

He barely heard what she'd said. A gust of wind brought her scent to him, and her features came to focus.

Lilliana Vargas.

A red-hot fury blazed through his veins, and he clenched his fingers around the handle of his gun. "You."

His animosity didn't make her retreat. Instead, she leaned toward him.

"Yeah, it's me, whoever you are. Now beat it." She dismissed him as if he were a human, possibly not recognizing him for the wolf she'd damn near electrocuted a couple of weeks ago in Cheese's cabin. Her jaw firmed despite the giant red welt and growing knot where she'd been hit. "I'm going inside."

He grabbed her arm. "No. You're not security. We've got to call my boss first."

She shook him free with a foul curse, and its creativity in calling into question his parentage drew a reluctant admiration from him. After she freed her hands and stepped several paces back, she said, "Whoever he is, he can't be here quickly enough. They're probably already transferring victims."

The wary determination in her eyes said he'd do little to dissuade her without putting a bullet in her head too. And though his whole body ached for days after whatever spell she'd hit him with, he couldn't find the desire to dish the same pain back to her.

Mouse appeared in Caleb's peripheral vision and formed the third point in a ninety-degree triangle. He must've sensed the tension—what wolf wouldn't?—because he kept his attention focused on the mage when he said, "Bound. Boss said CSS would be here in fifteen."

The mage's eyelids narrowed, and she stealthily dropped her hands behind her back. "I'm going in."

"So you said." Caleb widened his stance and prepared for battle. She probably hoped he hadn't seen her movement and even now primed spells in her hands.

"You're not going to stop me." Her shoulders tensed.

He hated both that she was right and he couldn't delay for much longer. "Besides the idea being monumentally stupid to go in alone, why would I let you?"

"Because my cousin may be in there." Her hands whipped out and sparking balls of energy zipped toward him and Mouse.

2

THE TWO MALES sprung aside to avoid Lilliana's immobility spells. Damn their speed. No fangs when they bared their teeth. Plus, they didn't have the sleek, European vibe of vampires or demons. They must be shifters.

Heart slamming against her ribs, she spun, scrambled onto the crumbling concrete dock, and raced for the padlocked door about midway down the building's side. A bright blare of light from behind her lit up the corrugated metal sheathing. She stifled a niggle of remorse at the potential hurt she could've caused if additional gargoyle guards found the shifter defenseless. Bah. She had bigger problems, getting inside being one.

Keep going. Shifters are quick. They'll be fine.

While she ran, she prepped an explosive spell in her palm. She tossed the crackling red ball at the door, following immediately with a sound-deadening spell. Just in time. With a bright flash, the corrugated metal door flew from its hinges.

She didn't bother worrying about the light. Normal humans could attribute the flare to kids' fireworks, sheet lightning on this humid night, a blown transformer, whatever, if they even saw the burst at after two in the morning.

Immobility spells primed in both hands, she darted through the door, curling around the jamb so her back pressed flat against the wall. While she sucked air in and out of her lungs, she pulled back the spell in one palm and conjured a lumiglow. She rolled the ball into the center to illuminate the interior.

No one stood sentry. No visible cameras in the ancient wood rafters. The guards wouldn't have attacked without something to protect. She scanned every inch of the building. It's fifty-yard interior hung with cobwebs, and a thick layer of dust lay on the occasional small trash pile, no doubt from kids looking for an escape or the homeless for a roof. A triangle of peachy-pink light slid onto the concrete floors at the other end of the building from a hole big enough to wiggle through. This probably accounted for the rubbish. Her evaluation took only moments.

Impatience bubbled in her blood. Had Merriwhether's expensive information been wrong? There had to be a door. *Duh. Hidden.* She directed her gaze around the building once more.

Boot scuffs echoed from outside, and she silently cursed. Those shifters could ruin everything. She needed to save her strength for the Underground, not fighting potentially good guys.

Her gaze darted around wildly while the light from her spell faded. Wait. Her focus snagged on a faint rectangle on the floor. While the markings could've been from an old closet which stood at one time, the outline also suggested...

A staircase.

She rushed over and placed her fingers on the floor, pleased with the surge of magical power that met her. She'd found the door.

Before the amulet she wore could fully disarm the ward, a rough hand hauled her to her feet.

She struggled against the being who held her. Anger clogged her ability to even emit actual words, and she bit back a threatening snarly wail. Manacles snapped around her wrists and prevented her from forming a spell. From the glimpses she caught, the arrogant, handsome, red-haired one restrained her. Damn his supernatural speed.

He shoved her against the wall, and she turned her face toward her target, barely visible in the lumiglow's fading light.

Suppressing a scream of frustration and fear for her cousin's fate, her gaze locked on the possible door. Her body seemed to writhe of its own accord in an attempt to break free.

The hard press of his body against hers rendered her virtually immobile against the wall's dusty, rough wood sheathing. The shifter's voice carried more than a hint of a growl. "What in the hell is wrong with you? You got a death wish or something?"

A shiver of apprehension shimmied down her spine with the warm breath against her ear. Her body tightened, and she found hauling air into her lungs even more difficult. She had to touch the bindings. These, too, probably carried the supposedly patented Santiago Systems spells, which nullified any paranormal ability of those who wore them. Her fingers met material. A...pants zipper placket.

Suddenly, air no longer became available to her. The hard body behind her held a strange familiarity, like she recognized his earthy, pine scent. Where had she encountered him before?

Focus! Anna might still be here. She tossed aside any need to know more about the shifter and returned to her reason for being here—rescue her cousin.

One of her family's wards protected the rectangular area, and therefore one she could disable with the amulet. Would the shifter care? Desperation added to the hot, angry knot rolling in her belly. She had to try.

Perhaps he'd release her if she used logic. "They wouldn't bother to guard this place if they weren't operating."

He didn't respond.

"And a security team wouldn't be here if they weren't looking for someone," she continued. "I found the access point and can get through the wards. If any of the Underground's victims are still here, those assholes are taking them to another location right now. We can't leave them behind."

He stilled against her, perhaps lessening his pressure a fraction. "You could get hurt."

Was a hint of intrigue in his tone? She ruthlessly pushed back a desire to wrestle against his hold. "No shit, Sherlock. I came alone."

Abruptly, his body's hard length disappeared, and she scrambled to pivot toward him. In the gloom, she couldn't make out much of him, other than his height, perhaps half a foot over her own five-foot-nine, and his outline spoke of wide, muscular shoulders and a narrow waist.

She touched the bindings. Definitely Santiago Systems cuffs. Mentally, she activated the counter spell, then she caught the manacles in her hand and pretended to remain restrained. No sense in alerting the shifter that she'd freed herself in case he wouldn't relent.

"I agree with your assessment. We'll go in. Mouse, did you hear that?" He paused, his gaze slightly unfocused, then nodded his head slightly. He must be talking to the other shifter. "Lemme know when the team or CSS shows. Dunno what we'll find down there."

Dammit. He'd called Clan Shifter Security.

He returned his gaze to her. "Alright. You can get through the wards. After that, we play by my rules."

"Look, dude—"

"Name's Caleb." He pulled something from the small of his back. By its shape, he held a gun, a very large automatic, and probably the one he'd been using earlier.

She wanted to shake her head with the way he took over the situation. "Look, *Caleb*, I am perfectly capa—"

"Have you been part of a dedicated building entry team or on NACS SWAT?" He paused. "I'll take your stare as a no." Though matter of fact, his tone bordered on rude. "Once we've broken through the wards, I'm going first. Do what I say, watch my six—my back—and we'll be okay. Agreed?"

"Fine." Like she had a choice? She'd been going on emotion since she'd gotten the information Anna might be held here. Her rational side said he made sense.

"Let's get those cuffs off you."

She brought her arms from behind her back, bindings in one hand. She offered them to him without the smirk attempting to burst through. "I may not be NACS SWAT, but I have skills."

He opened his mouth, possibly to ask how she freed herself, then shook his head, a smaller version of how a dog might shake off stress. He took the cuffs and tucked them in his tactical pants' thigh pocket. "You got a gun?"

"No. Never needed one." She wiggled her fingers at him and generated a shower of sparks. Well, maybe when her confidence wavered her spells could go wonky, but that's why she chose accounting, not Clan Magic Security.

"Know how to handle firearms?" After she jerked her chin to indicate "yes," he reached behind his back and then produced a twin to the gun he held in his other hand. He offered the pistol to her. "Here. Safety's off, and she's ready to go."

Lilliana stopped herself from saying she didn't like guns, that her spells were just fine. But she'd adopted this badass role. She needed to keep up the charade. Luckily, her uncle, the owner of Santiago Systems, showed her how to shoot and taught her the cardinal rules of firearms safety a couple of years ago.

In response to his question about handling firearms, she said, "Finger off the trigger and outside the trigger guard until ready to shoot, et cetera."

"Good." She didn't think it possible, but his gaze grew more serious. "Got a flashbang thing like the one you used outside? We need the light and the noise."

"Yes." Here she felt a little more confident. So far, so good with her notoriously unreliable spell casting. Her nerves jittered, but she'd not gone wonky yet.

"Open the door and drop one in. Then we're going in fast and hard. Since you'll be looking backward, try to hold onto my shirt's collar or backpack so you can keep up."

"Got it." An impatient yet nervous energy rippled across her while he followed her to the outline on the floor.

She knelt and slapped her free hand on the ward, praying her uncle hadn't added a recent update which invalidated the amulet. While she worked the reversal, the outline sparked and shimmered but no harm came to her. Relief sagged the tension in her shoulders by a small amount.

Within a couple of seconds, she'd revealed a descending staircase. Without any lighting, a black abyss appeared to yaw before her. She shivered. Using a lumiglow wouldn't be prudent, and she couldn't see as well as the shifter.

The impending danger made her heart race and breathing jump. She cataloged the reaction as adrenaline while she primed the explosive spell and tossed it in. Hurriedly, she plugged an ear with her finger. The other hand was occupied with the weapon, and one ear would just have to do.

A second later came the flash and a boom that rattled the metal building and her brain. A little bigger than she wanted, but the shifter seemed unfazed.

"Go."

Luckily, the one ear wasn't ringing so she could hear his word. With shaking fingers, she grabbed the handle on top of his Santiago-logoed backpack and raced after him, scanning over her shoulders for any threats.

She stumbled once on the stairs because of her clunky boots, and she caught herself before she tumbled. The darkness closed around her such that she couldn't see anything, though for some reason, maybe the way her harsh breaths echoed, she believed they'd entered a tunnel.

Ugh. The scent of pee and shit met her nose. She must be in the right place. The Underground treated its captives—all female and all valuable in their own paranormal way—like animals.

From her slight contact with Caleb, she could tell when he reached level ground. She twisted her body so that she pointed the weapon behind her consistently and strained her eyesight for any movement. Not quite running, but not walking either, she moved quickly with him. The position and speed were awkward as hell. Better than doing this alone though.

She'd never been in this situation. Could she really kill someone if needed? How much longer would they go before finding anything, even opposition? Tension climbed up her neck.

After what felt like an hour but could've only been about ten seconds, the smell became stronger, the darkness began to lift, and she could make out her surroundings, a tunnel with rough, cement block walls.

A gunshot sounded, making her heart stutter in her chest, and she almost released her grip on Caleb's backpack. Two more loud reports came quickly after. Was that a grunt? Had someone been killed? Her palm became slick and she tightened her fingers around the gun so the hard plastic didn't slip from her hand.

He stopped, then started again.

What was going on? She didn't dare leave their backs exposed like he'd directed, so she kept her focus on the way she'd entered. More gunshots. Her hand began to shake from the gun's weight and her worry.

"Hands up, asshole." Caleb's order was sharp and mean.

She risked a glance over her shoulder. A large room lined with cages met her gaze, some still with victims inside, some empty, doors hanging open.

None were Anna. A cold anger blasted through her system followed by an icing of despair. Would she ever find her cousin?

Focus. You can still save the others. The words seemed to come in her grandmother's voice.

Lilliana continued to take in her surroundings. Two males of an undetermined clan lay on the ground.

Over Caleb's broad shoulder, she caught the sandy-blond hair and one eye of a male in the far corner. She'd know the carefully styled mane anywhere.

Derwin.

Her mouth dried with her fury. Even though she'd suspected him as part of the conspiracy, his presence still stung.

How could she have consented to be the fiancée of the arrogant, abusive jerk of a mage?

Caleb slid to the left a little, shielding his body's presence with the hallway's corner.

She quickly followed, but not before she caught that the tall, whipcord thin mage stood next to a personal portal he'd created, a scowl on his features, and a gun in one hand pointed at the shifter.

Derwin pulled the trigger.

3

WHEN CALEB FIRED his gun at the mage ahead of him, Lilliana screamed. Almost simultaneously, the bullet smacked into his abdomen nearly as hard as one of Mouse's punches. Pain stabbed his far-left side, nothing critical for now.

Then the spell from the bullet hit his neurons, and a white-hot blaze threatened to overwhelm him. The round didn't merely deliver excruciating agony. Assuming this was a normal spelled round, the devilish magic ensured delayed self-healing, a gift given to most paranormals.

Fuck.

Hebert Security and NACS weren't the only ones to lay out for the best in spelled bullets. By the agony, this was a Santiago Systems product. He walled off his response with the same sheer force of will he used to ignore the stench of piss, shit, blood, and fear in this room. This wasn't the first time he'd been tagged by a spelled round. He'd certainly prefer for it to be his last.

While he'd received a minor wound, a dark splotch on the

mage's chest, maybe middle left lung, stained his shirt. He stumbled toward the personal portal and was going to escape.

Not if Caleb could stop him.

Gritting his teeth against the pain, Caleb moved forward, tapping his trigger twice. He landed at least one more round, possibly to the head by the way the male flopped forward, but he'd fallen into his portal, which closed with a distinctive *pop*.

Shit. He kept scanning for threats, but none appeared, much to his relief. The fire in his left side flamed again, and he involuntarily sucked in a sharp breath, only managing to disturb the wound, creating yet more agony. He doubled down on the mental wall he built against the pain. Though he had several Mend Me potions in his backpack, the victims and Lilliana came first.

"You okay back there?"

"Yep."

Was that a tremor in her tone? A click and a question in his ear through the communications device interrupted further inquiry. Mouse needed a sit-rep.

"Two Underground goons down." Caleb scanned the cages and the three females inside who were silent but appeared otherwise unharmed. "Three victims remaining. Unknown number of victims transported out. Hit a mage, but he portaled and escaped. I took one, but it's minor."

"Ten-four. CSS is about five out. Should I ask them for a courtesy call to Magic Security?"

"We'll work on extracting the victims. I think I've got a ringer here." Usually, it took someone from Clan Magic Security to break the spell used on the cages. Lilliana broke through the ward on the door to this basement and the spelled cuffs he'd put on her. She probably would make short work of any security measures that made the barred cells into formidable containers for all manner of paranormal beings.

Before he asked for her help, he risked a glance over his shoulder to where she waited, still covering their six. Most would've been caught up in the room's scene, but she maintained focus. Not bad for someone untrained in building entry. "Cover me."

Her dark brown gaze met his, and she jerked a nod. Before he could tell her to take a position at the hallway-room transition where she could watch for threats from both areas, she moved into the position. She had the gun in one hand, a crackling red spell in the other. "Got it."

Thank God she hadn't turned into a puddle. Although why he would think she might have a soft side mystified him considering how she'd attacked him a couple of weeks ago as well as him and Mouse today.

He shoved his gun into the holster strapped to his thigh, then reached behind to the handcuffs secured to the outside of his backpack and pulled one from its quick-release moorings.

In short order, he bound both downed Underground members. One had the light features and distinctive, otherworldly odor of a fae. The other smelled of shifter and had a white streak in his hair. Ugh. The musk. Weasel for sure, possibly even a honey badger. Good thing he'd taken out the guy before a fight. Those shifters didn't give up, and it sometimes took a whole wolf pack to subdue them. Luckily, the bindings shrank or expanded to fit the captive. Otherwise, Caleb would've required two sets to fit the muscle-bound mustelid.

Since these two weren't from Clan Magic, the cuffs should work for the time being. He'd need to return his batch and let them know someone had figured out a way around their spell system. Weird since they usually had an excellent reputation for invulnerability.

Once he'd completed the task, he stepped away from the unconscious prisoners. The wounds would hurt like the fires of hell, but both would be nursed back to health. Then they'd be turned over to NACS for prosecution, though not before CSS had an interrogation crack at them.

"Calf rope," he said, then realized she may not understand his terminology. "They're secure."

"Okay." Her firm tone and even breathing said she'd gotten over her earlier jitters. Hard to fool a shifter when he could hear an elevated heart rate or smell the pheromones pushed out by fear.

He redrew his gun and stepped to the corner opposite Lilliana. She'd flipped a switch to illuminate the passage. Smart. He'd worked exclusively with shifters for a decade, and he'd forgotten not every paranormal being could see in the virtual dark. "I'll take the hallway if you think you can get the cells open. Or should we call Clan Magic Security?"

He risked a glance to her.

She stared at the captives with a confident smirk on her features, then her gaze flashed to his. "I got it."

Maybe he'd figured this woman all wrong. She wasn't the asshole he'd suspected when he first encountered her in Cheese's cabin. He stretched out his hand. "Give me the gun, then get to it. I'll cover you."

She handed the weapon to him, then turned, only to whip her head back with a gasp. "You've been shot."

The agony threatened to resume with the reminder, and he ground his teeth. "I'm fine."

For a moment, she paused. Then she came closer and held

up her hands, both covered with a swirling blue aura. "This won't hurt, but it will dull the pain."

Before he could comment that nothing but Mend Me and time could work on a spelled bullet, she'd cupped her hands over both sides of his wound, a through-and-through just above his waistband.

What in the hell? The agony had receded to mere pain, the same ache as when his body began to naturally repair itself and not the inferno the spelled bullet left behind. His synapses almost wept with relief.

She stepped back, and his gaze collided with hers. "How did you do that?"

With a half-smile he couldn't decipher, she turned to the cells. "We can talk later. Gotta get these ladies free."

However much he wanted to pull her aside and demand to know how she'd countered a spell that was considered in the paranormal world to be a guarantee of prolonged torment, the victims were more important. He wanted to observe her work, but he needed to ensure no one approached or entered through magical means, so he focused on his priority.

A *snick* followed by an immediate grate of metal on metal caught his attention and he flicked a glance over his shoulder.

Already Lilliana had stepped to the next cell, but the first one's door had swung wide. The petite woman who'd been contained inside stepped to the opening and halted as if not quite trusting the opening truly existed. She flipped her long, silver braid over her shoulder, then straightened the rumpled T-shirt she wore atop her jeans, which had been stained with dark streaks appearing suspiciously like dried blood. The woman shot an unfathomable glance to Lilliana, who'd already set to work at the second cage.

The faintest thumps of multiple footsteps sounded overhead, while behind him came another *snick* and metallic grating, followed by sniffs and soft sobs. Lilliana murmured words of comfort. Boot-falls rumbled on the stairs and "Coming in," boomed down the hallway.

Good. Mouse could cover that area. Caleb turned his full focus to Lilliana and the remaining victims. "It's going to be okay, ladies. Investigators are on their way down."

"Screw that." The soft words had barely been spoken before the pop of a personal portal echoed in the room.

He shifted his focus toward the sound. "No. Wait."

His words came too late. The petite female—obviously a level one mage if she could summon a portal—stepped through and closed her escape route before he could stop her. All he saw before the oval closed was rough brick and black pavement. The stench of rotting garbage added to the miasma of the underground room.

Though frustrated she left, he couldn't blame her. Testifying against a group of people who kidnapped and killed for a living often ended poorly for the victim. Bastards.

Another pop sounded behind him, and he swung his weapon to the threat.

He met Lilliana's gaze, and she firmed her generous lips into a hard line.

She stepped through her portal and was gone.

4

LILLIANA PUT the empty vial of foul-tasting Mend-Me potion onto the coffee table, then popped the peppermint that came with the purchase into her mouth. *Gross.* With a sigh, she flopped onto her living room's couch and laid her head against a throw pillow.

The disgusting taste of the elixir was the least of her problems.

Exhaustion beat at her body, begging her to rest, not unlike the heartbeat pounding in her cheek. She'd never been punched before, let alone by a gargoyle. The potion should allow for the pain to recede. But her undercover mission left little time for sleep. According to Merriwhether, the word on the street was the Underground's auction approached. If she couldn't find Anna before they sold her off like a farm implement, Lilliana might never find her cousin. Sure, the witch could be a little annoying at times. Plus, she probably needed a quick kick in the pants to continue college. Didn't mean she deserved a life of slavery, forced to create whatever potion or charm—legal or illegal—her master desired.

Lilliana stared at the faint, sweeping patterns in the ceiling's plaster. Unfortunately, the swirls didn't randomly coalesce into words and answer the questions that circled in her mind as if borne by a tornado.

Had Merriwhether given her the correct information—where the Underground held Anna? Or was he just giving her anything he found without being reasonably assured of the veracity? He was a dwarf after all, though he wouldn't have his reputation as one of the best intelligence sources in all of North America if he sold people bogus information. Perhaps he believed Lilliana could only afford that single, exorbitant payment, one which would've wiped out her entire savings? If Clan Magic Security hadn't footed the bill, Lilliana couldn't have met the dwarf's price.

And if he *had* been right, if Anna *had* been held in that miserable hole, where had they taken her? Correction, where had Derwin and his asshole buddies taken her?

She was pretty sure he hadn't recognized her, since she got a mere glimpse with one eye over the shifter's shoulder. Still, she should've taken a new ID potion or worn a concealment amulet.

Rage formed an icy ball in her stomach. The miserable snake couldn't have gone far, since even the most powerful mages could travel only about twenty miles per portal. She was one of the few that could travel almost twenty-five, the only sure thing about her unpredictable magic and a source of pride for her.

Derwin? He could only travel about ten, even less tonight since the shifter shot him. He'd never make his home in Illusion. At over one hundred miles between Elgin and the hidden Clan Magic city, Derwin would use every drop of magical energy with the number of personal portals he'd have to form and still only travel a tenth of the needed the distance. He'd probably go to another Underground holding area.

Finally, Lilliana's remaining questions would no longer be ignored. Who was the shifter?

The undeniable sense she'd met him before pricked at her memory. The color of his hair, new-penny copper, had never been her type, but it fit him and his lean, muscular length. His fragrance, like fresh pine, newly sawn oak, and musk, had invaded her senses almost to the point where she could no longer smell the fetid, stinking holding area. And when she'd brushed against his pants' placket, a fleeting desire shot through her and dared her to find what lay beyond the zipper.

Lilliana rubbed her gritty eyes. The stupid and inappropriate thought, no matter how brief, must be from her lack of pillow time. She could use the same excuse for her offer to heal the shifter. But his desire to help, only to end up shot, tugged at her sympathy. Dumb. She jeopardized everything she'd accomplished with Clan Magic Security.

In fact, she should call Detective Slocomb right now with the results, which were zero where her cousin was concerned. The investigator had approached her several weeks ago to help with Smoke Roundtree's crew, saying they heard he might be involved with Anna's disappearance, though the intel didn't pan out. Then last week they'd asked her to do some snooping. They'd explained their suspicions about her uncle's claim his daughter had been kidnapped by the Underground. The two had logically laid out the inconsistencies in Tío Manny's story and despite liking her uncle, Lilliana agreed to help.

Any betrayal she experienced from poking around her uncle's warehouse and office had evaporated tonight when the amulet she found hidden in a secret compartment in his desk worked on the ward. Since she'd come to work as a mole in her uncle's firm, she noticed several subtle irregularities in spells' formulations and ward components.

Tío, a witch who had married into the Vargas family of influential mages, used his powers to craft wards sold by his company. But he could only create wards, amulets, potions, and charms. To round out his security business, he'd partnered with Derwin Stanford for the mage's ability to both create and cast spells.

She should've believed her grandmother. *No good comes from mixing magical classes.* Bah. She pushed aside the older woman's unwelcome discriminatory words, as well as why the attractive shifter seemed to prowl around the edges of her thoughts like a wolf keeping to the tree line, waiting to ambush his prey.

Call Detective Slocomb. Her stomach protested with a loud growl. Okay, food first. Then she'd report in to the clan security officer.

She rose, and her bones felt heavy, as if the weight of her part in rescuing her cousin wanted to drag her back to the comfortable couch. Not yet. Once she'd done everything she could, she would take a well-deserved vacation from work, maybe to Hawaii. The sun would feel good. When was the last time she'd actually relaxed anyway?

She could've warmed the frozen meal herself, but the effort would've expended too much energy considering some of her remaining power was used to fix her cheek. The apartment's tiny kitchen had a microwave, which would do just as good a job.

While the appliance worked its own brand of magic, she filled a glass from the tap and greedily sucked down the water, not caring if her bladder would cry for release in only a couple of hours. She glanced at the clock. She needed to be getting up for work anyway by then. Her uncle would expect her promptly at eight.

The food could've used a bit more time to cook, but her eyelids insisted they wouldn't stay open for much longer. She shoved the food in her mouth mechanically and not at all with what her grandmother might've called "manners." *Chew, girl,* echoed in her head, but she ignored the acid voice. While she wolfed down her dinner, she considered the shifter once more.

With certainty, she'd never seen him in Illusion, where she grew up. The clan had too tight a magical control on its borders to let in strays. She hadn't met him through her family, either, since they frowned on fraternizing with anyone not of Clan Magic blood. Her memories turned muzzy, and she couldn't seem to focus any longer.

Gah. Her stupid physical reaction and where she'd encountered him would resolve once she'd gotten some sleep.

The tiny tray didn't take long to empty, and after the last bite, Lilliana dumped it along with her fork and glass into the sink. With each passing second, her body seemed more weighed down, and each step became an intense effort.

At least her apartment was small. She struggled through the bedroom door, then tripped courtesy of her boot's toe stubbing on the carpet. So bone-weary, her mind didn't process at first that she should break her fall. If she had to faceplant, at least she landed on her bed. She lay there for a moment.

Some badass mage I am... Damn boot... I should... call...Detective...

An insistent banging caused her to jerk upright. Heart pounding like a troll's hammer, her gaze darted around the room, trying to orient herself. Light streamed in through the blinds at an intensely bright angle. She caught a glimpse of her bedside clock.

Oh shit. Ten. She was supposed to be at Santiago Systems two hours ago. For a moment, the shock of having overslept so badly froze her in place.

The pounding started again, only this time, her uncle shouted in his deep, booming tone, "Lilliana, are you in there?"

The violence perpetrated against her door and the volume of Manny's voice broke her inaction. She jumped to her feet. Which were still in boots. Oh, hell. She'd slept in the tactical gear from last night. With a wave of her hand, she removed the black boots, cargo pants, and long-sleeve T-shirt, then quickly donned her favorite corgi pajamas. The robe came next. Finally, she stepped into a set of well-worn fuzzy slippers set just so next to her bed.

The mirror over her dresser said she wouldn't have to muss her hair. Her janked-up ponytail was real, just like the deep crease across her cheek from where she must've laid across a big seam. At least the contusion from the gargoyle had cleared.

She moved toward the hallway past her dresser and caught a flash at her neck in the mirror. Wait. She tucked the amulets she wore under the neck of her shirt, including the one she'd "borrowed" from her uncle's desk, then tugged the robe's lapels together. Hustling into the main room, she tried to cobble a reasonable story together using brain cells that were currently working in panic mode.

When her uncle began another round of jackhammer-style knocking, she began to worry her neighbors might think something was wrong. Once she'd broken up with Derwin, she moved outside Illusion and into the human economy where the rents were cheaper. If Tío Manny tried to use magic to get inside her apartment, there'd be hell to pay, the least of which would be from the clan.

"I'm coming," she yelled while she made the short trek to the door. What to tell him?

Sick. She'd caught something—goodness knew what—because she'd been working herself silly to fulfill all of the Santiago Systems orders and at her regular day job. Yeah. That's it. Like she'd been instructed, she hadn't told anyone she'd been granted a leave of absence a couple of weeks ago to try to help Clan Magic Security find Anna.

Just tell Tío you need to see a healer and grab a remedy at Belladonna Apothecary or something. From her earlier glance in the mirror, her eyes were already red-rimmed and puffy. She rubbed her nose to make the tip rosy and a bit swollen, then prepared to affect a tone akin to a cold.

She deactivated the wards embedded in the door, then removed the spells she'd laid on top last night. Once she'd learned the supposedly impenetrable Santiago wards had an amulet as a built-in back door, she'd been sure to put an additional spell defense layer on top. Even though she didn't think Derwin recognized her before he was shot, she needed to take precautions.

When she swung the panel open, Tío Manny stood with his hands on his wide hips, square chin thrust froward. The witch always reminded her of a perpetually exhausted bulldog, short legs, barrel chest, and a head like a bucket. A mother of five teen bear shifters could fit her weekly groceries in the bags under his eyes. Today, the faint but still repulsive scent of bryony clung to him. He'd obviously been working with stones used to intensify wards. Ugh. Like the one at the warehouse last night.

"Good morning, Tío. I'm sorry I'm late. I must've slept through my alarm." She added a nasal whine to her words. Would he buy her schtick? He needed her, so even if he thought she was faking, he still might want her to continue at his business.

"You're sick?" His gaze narrowed on her, perhaps because paranormals rarely got a simple cold or flu. But she'd hunched her shoulders a bit and crossed her arms, topping the body language with as miserable an expression on her features as possible.

Dammit. You can convince him. You've been acting your whole life. She made a big show of wiping her sleeve at her nose. What had she heard while at the grocery in Illusion the other day? She said with a nasal mumble, "Some sort of gremlin virus has been going around."

He stepped back almost to the other side of the narrow breezeway. "Steve's kids had that. You better not have infected the office."

She curled her shoulders in a little more. "I just started feeling bad last night when I left work around midnight. No one was there after five-thirty anyway."

"Fine, but you know with us being down a mage since Derwin resigned, and since..." His mouth pursed as if he bit back a painful memory.

When he mentioned her ex, she fought back the rage and struggled to maintain her role.

"We're all having to pull double duty," he continued. "I need you at Santiago Systems." His tone had grown stern, like she was a kid playing sick and not wanting to go to school.

She wanted to explode with her knowledge, to tell her uncle

just why Derwin left the company, what he'd done to the products, and she knew damn well that his departure wasn't for a better paying job at a competitor. That she knew Tío was up to something with the Underground, and it somehow involved why his daughter, Anna, had been kidnapped two weeks ago.

Instead of blurting all of that out, she asked, "Have we heard anything from Detective Slocomb about Anna?"

"Nothing. He said they were still hopeful she could be recovered. But..." Tío's lips firmed. "I shouldn't get my hopes up."

Lilliana faked her sympathetic expression. "Are you sure you don't want to try to find an investigation agency to help?"

His lower jaw jutted, and if possible, the bags under his eyes sagged even more. "They said they'd kill her. I'm not going to risk my Anna."

Like whatever fate his daughter faced wouldn't be worse than death anyway. Though Anna was a beautiful woman, the Underground would only care about her magical abilities. She was especially good with charms. Using magic to actively harm another instead of defense would be against all she'd been taught.

Guilt snagged at Lilliana's conscience. She should've been up and at her uncle's production facility to snoop, not playing hooky today. Once more, she swiped at her nose then added what she hoped sounded like a realistic cough. "I'll head directly to Belladonna Apothecary to see if they have anything. That'll cut down the wait for a healer who will tell me what I already am pretty sure I've got."

His shoulders drooped, and he rubbed a hand over his face. "I'm sorry, *mi sobrina*. It's just gotten busy lately and with Anna..."

A couple of weeks ago, she might've pulled him into a big

hug and told him everything would be okay. Now? Nope. "I'm sorry, Tío. I'll let you know when the potion is supposed to be in effect. Hopefully, I'll be there later today."

While she'd love to sleep the day away, she needed to learn everything she could, including his betrayal, if she was to find his daughter.

5

CALEB PULLED his SUV into the empty Santiago Systems parking lot. Huh. He glanced at the clock on the dash, which said two-fifty. He checked his phone where the site said they were open Sundays until three. Must be a slow day, or they closed early.

Last duty of the trip was to return the faulty bindings he'd put on Lilliana two nights ago. His boss was none too pleased to have a received a bum shipment of cuffs. Mistakes like that could cause someone their life. Luckily, the mage hadn't wanted to roast him alive like she nearly had a couple of weeks ago. Since Santiago charged a premium for the word "inescapable" in the item's description, along with a lifetime warranty, they should replace the set for free.

After he put his vehicle in park and turned the engine off, Caleb rubbed his face, weary in every fiber, bone, and neuron.

What a weekend. Yesterday had been full of debriefings, first by Clan Shifter Security, then by Clan Magic Security, then by North American Council Security. His ass still smarted from the seemingly endless hours in the hard, plastic chairs, and his stomach remained soured from the seemingly bottomless cups of thick, strong coffee.

Fortunately, one of the females they'd rescued two nights ago was the one Hebert Security had been hired to find. At least lucky for Lilliana. She'd messed up the surveillance, and according to one of the women, five more had been transported out. While he was still pissed the mage forced his and Mouse's hand and interrupted the opportunity to rescue more, at least he'd been able to count the mission an overall success.

He rubbed his belly. Hopefully, he'd have time for a well-deserved steak at The Werehouse before his scheduled vortex trip from Enchanted Rock to the Peigneur vortex in Louisiana. The meal would make the next day of office paperwork bearable. If he hadn't lost a coin flip to Mouse, he'd be chowing down right now, which was undoubtedly what his partner was doing, lucky bastard.

Caleb approached the main door of the unassuming warehouse that had been spelled to appear to be about the size of a three-bedroom house built of corrugated metal. He yanked on the door and was surprised it swung open. Inside, the small vestibule had a single door with a sign printed in simple block letters that said, "Please wait here, we will be with you in a moment." He'd been here before and knew the routine. Several seconds later, the wards recognized his shifter blood.

The slightest *click* heralded the door in front of him opening. He stepped into the horseshoe-shaped showroom, where bright lights reflected off the undoubtedly spelled, pure quartz lining the standing display cases, as well as the ones built into the walls.

Strange. Usually, there was an attendant, if not Santiago himself, behind the counter. Caleb glanced to the door set midway down the wall to his right. Though someone might mistake the panel for flimsy, hollow-core construction, he knew better than to try to open it and call out they had a customer. About five years ago, a group broke into the facility, then got greedy and tried to get more from the warehouse in back. Not only did whatever magic Santiago used to protect his goods keep the intruders completely contained, the spell or ward or whatever caused every nerve in their body a debilitating pain until the magic was disabled. No one had tried a heist since.

"I'll be there in a minute," said a woman's voice.

He lifted his gaze in the direction from where the staticky, tinny words had emanated. Where two walls and the ceiling converged, he located a small speaker with a glint of what must be a built-in camera. He set the faulty cuffs on the glass across from the door, then went over to the case containing the backpacks about the size he'd see a teen using for school but that had been spelled to carry far more cargo within. Two nights ago, he'd used one he got a couple years back, a medium-sized version, and one without the costly add-on of a weight negation spell. As a shifter, he usually could manage what he needed to carry, though sometimes it'd be nice to not bear the weight. He'd been saving his money for the deluxe model, the one with the largest capacity plus the ability to not to be burdened with loads of gear.

The door opened behind him, and he turned to where a woman backed herself into the showroom, arms full with a large box.

The door swung shut behind her, and she pivoted.

Caleb froze and took in the person's form. If her scent hadn't confirmed this was indeed Lilliana, he might've discounted his own vision.

Her long, dark hair fell over her shoulder from where she'd

bound the strands at her nape. A bright pink T-shirt hugged her torso. The two-line logo in black stretched across her breasts and read, "Santiago Systems--When You Care to Spell Your Very Best." Dark smudges on the knit fabric suggested she did more than just work in the showroom. Worn, faded jeans hugged her hips and would no doubt highlight her pert ass.

His wolf let out a howl at the memory of her wiggling against him. He fought through the infernal noise to the idea that she worked here.

She hefted the box onto the counter then brought her gaze up to his with a polite salesperson crescent on her lips. "What can I..." Her lower jaw hung open, and her eyes widened before she shut her mouth with a snap. If her spine became any stiffer, he would've thought it a steel pipe. She recovered her polite demeanor quickly. "What can I help you with?"

Pretend to not recognize me?

He prowled back across the short distance and kept his gaze locked with hers. When she inhaled sharply and lifted her chin, a short laugh threatened to burst from him. Mercifully, he kept his features schooled into the same slightly mocking countenance. He stopped in front of her, the sales case between them the only thing keeping him from walking her backward until his thighs mingled with hers.

While the silence stretched between them, he pushed his wolf back repeatedly. The stupid animal didn't seem to care. Finally, he said, "Hello Lilliana. I was here to report to someone that the bindings had a security flaw."

She swallowed hard, and she darted a glance to the corner of the ceiling where the speaker/camera combo perched. When she brought her gaze to his once more, pleading had replaced the aloofness in her features.

What was going on here?

"Uh, hi." The hesitation in her tone matched the fear pheromones falling from her in waves. "They're probably just faulty. I'll replace them for you."

She reached out to pick up the cuffs, but he quickly covered her hand, trapping her fingers against the counter. He leaned in and whispered, "Why were you able to get out of them?"

The panic in her eyes when she darted them from him to the camera created a smidgeon of pity, but when she threw back her shoulders and firmed her lips, any compassion dissolved.

She yanked her hand out from under his, bringing the bindings with her. She tucked the metal restraints into her back jeans pocket. "Like I said, the spell must've been faulty."

Uh huh. She'd also bypassed the wards on the door and whatever spell, ward, or combo thereof Santiago used to secure the cages. If the spell had merely been faulty, he was a troll. "Can your uncle have someone test them?"

She crossed her arms. "I'm the only mage in the building."

"Then I'd like to talk to him." Manny Santiago needed to know someone—Lilliana—had defeated his supposedly undefeatable magical products.

She took a couple of steps down the counter, opened the back of one of the display cases, and removed a box. "There's no one but me here right now."

"Really."

"My uncle left ten minutes ago. Here's a new set." She set the box, labeled "All-Clan binding" and branded with the company logo, on the counter hard enough that the metal cuffs inside clanked loudly. With a steely glare, she approached a door built into the counter system. She passed through the wicket, then opened the exit into the vestibule. "Now, if you'll leave, I need to lock up."

His wolf chuffed several times with her this close, and his entire being came to attention. *Not the time to be a horndog.* Once he'd shoved his feral awareness aside, he stared at her for several long seconds. He hadn't mistaken her earlier—she was hiding something. He hardened his tone and said, "Then I'll just have to come in tomorrow to speak with him."

She caught her lower lip between her teeth. And there was that fear pheromone again, stronger this time.

Something was going on. With the way she kept stealing glances to the camera, he had to get her out of this place to get any answers.

He crossed swiftly to her, and she took several steps until her one of the cases stopped her retreat. Her wide eyes spoke of fear but then she held up her hands and said, "Stop."

The swirling balls of energy she held advised him to do as she ordered. But then he'd never really been good at taking advice or doing as ordered, so...

He crowded her close and murmured, "I'm not going to hurt you."

If anything, the swirling balls became brighter though the fear on her features had turned to wariness.

"I know something is going on you don't want the people who are monitoring the camera in the corner to know."

The telltale flick of her gaze said he'd scored a direct hit. He smothered a dart of satisfaction. "Either you meet me, and we talk elsewhere, or I'm showing up here tomorrow."

Her whole body tensed, then she whispered, "Where?"

Moderately surprised she agreed, he quickly thought of a spot. "Your place?"

"No. Somewhere public."

While his feral side wanted her all to himself, he understood her distrust. "I need to eat, and you look like you could stand a good meal. How about The Werehouse at Enchanted Rock. This place closes at three. Say four-thirty?" It would take him about a half hour to get back to the Rock, then he needed to change. He shook himself. Why did he want to look good for her?

A yip in the back of his mind made him want to roll his eyes. *Down boy*.

She nibbled at her lower lip once more. The fear aroma had abated, and now her natural scent dominated, one of vanilla and rose, filling his nose and his lungs with her intriguing fragrance.

"Okay. I can make it." She narrowed her lids and compressed her lips. "But no funny business."

He almost laughed at the old-fashioned cliché. "Deal. And don't be late, Lilliana." He turned abruptly and strode through the door without a backward glance.

"Wait..." Her racing feet pattered after him. Concerned she'd decided to cancel their deal, he continued through the vestibule and had made it to the far side of his vehicle before she threw open the business's outside door. "How did you know my name?"

"I'll see you at four-thirty. If you tell me the truth, I'll tell you how I know you."

6

Lilliana straightened the hem of the slightly see-through, swiss-dot lace blouse. With a little turn, she checked her backside in the dressing room mirror. *Nice.*

Why did she care what her ass looked like anyway? She'd only come into to Boutique Magique in Enchanted Rock because she didn't have time to go to her apartment and change. A dirty shop T-shirt, jeans, and sneakers weren't something she would wear to even meet with her best friend, who just happened to be Thelma, the shop's owner.

"I bet that combo looks great, Lills," the sorcerer singsonged through the curtain.

"Yeah, T, it kind of does." She pushed the top's hem into her waistband and centered the thin belt's buckle. Her friend thrust a pair of strappy black sandals between the curtain and the wall. "These will make your legs look longer than a giraffe shifter's."

The sky-high stilettos were far out of Lilliana's wheelhouse. She'd fall and twist her ankle for sure. Flats and sensible mid-heels for important events were much more her style.

"Before you hand them back, they're spelled to not allow you to fall, twist your ankle, or be the cause of hurting yourself in any way." T's tone held dry laughter. "Plus, a quick triple tap on the small label under the arch turns them into Chuck high-tops, complete with socks. A triple tap on the sneaker's outside logo turns them back into the sandals."

Lilliana stared at the gorgeous shoes dangling from her fingers, then turned them over to view the label in the arch. The small piece of innocuous plastic provided her size—nine and a half. Why had she never thought of spelling shoes? She couldn't deny the heels would be sleek paired with the tapered-leg, black jeans. Nothing to do now but try them on.

She sat on the stool's edge and slipped her feet inside.

"Who's this guy you're meeting? Not that twerp, Derwin." The sorcerer's voice had grown suspicious with the last sentence.

Lilliana fumbled with the last buckle. She hated not divulging everything to her best friend, from Anna's predicament to Derwin's treachery to the shifter she was about to meet. But Detective Slocomb said not to tell anyone. Once Lilliana finished, she stood and swept the curtain to the side. "No, not Derwin."

"Wow." T's mouth stayed in the "O" shape at the end of her word, and her gaze gave her friend a good once-over. "You look dark, dangerous, and delicious. Whoever this mystery man is, he's going to want to eat you up whole."

Lilliana almost lied, but she couldn't do that to her best and only friend. "Nope. It's a shifter." Lilliana's obscenely wealth family was firmly in the marry-another-mage-for-social-standing camp, not unlike many in their stratified world. They would've freaked out if she married a witch, like her aunt had with Tío, and thereby 'sullying' her family with that of a "lower class" within Clan Magic. A shifter would make them apoplectic.

A small smirk popped onto T's lips. "Since it's a shifter, I hope it's a wolf shifter and that you're having a fun fling to get over that enema named Derwin. Or are you finally ready to break free of your family's expectations?"

Ugh. Lilliana shouldn't have said anything. She almost pulled the curtain back and changed into her old clothing so she could head home. This was ridiculous. But she'd agreed to meet this Caleb—a shifter, no less. Why? Because he knew who she was. Though, with the internet nowadays, probably anyone could've figured out her identity.

She chewed her lip before she reminded herself to stop the bad habit. Not only had he called her by name, but he intimated the bindings weren't actually faulty, meaning he probably figured out there was a way to compromise the magic. Not good for the investigation. The less who knew the better according to Detective Slocomb.

Of course the shifter would figure out the secret when the holding cages were Santiago Systems. The ward shielding the staircase to the underground holding area was also Santiago Systems. The round which had hit him was spelled by Santiago Systems.

She wanted to slap herself upside the back of her head for being so slow and stupid. Usually her friends considered her quite brilliant. Sleep. She needed more sleep.

Though she'd kill for a nap, she couldn't have him tell her uncle. Not when so much was riding on getting her cousin back and trying to figure out if Tío Manny was indeed involved. The family name would be toast. She cut the thought short. Now she sounded like her grandmother.

"Hey, Lills, you okay?"

She shook herself free from her dark thoughts and met her friend's concerned gaze in the mirror. "I'm sorry. What?"

"I said, I'm going to put some makeup on you and fix your hair a bit."

"I'm fine." Lilliana straightened her ponytail.

"You *are* fine." T's tone carried a hint of deadpan. "In fact, you're naturally quite pretty, but with this outfit, you need gorgeous. Close your eyes." Thelma snapped her fingers. "Look, Lills."

She cracked her lids, then opened them wide. Her chestnut hair cascaded over her shoulders, straight and sleek, even though she hadn't time to wash it in the last two days. Not a hint of frizz or ponytail elastic crimp marred the satin fall. And her face. Holy hell. The smokey shadow made her brown eyes sultry, while the rest of the makeup's subtleness merely enhanced what she'd been given in the genetic lottery, which for most paranormals was usually pretty damn good looking anyway.

Doubt assailed her once more. Why did she need to look this good for a meeting? To impress the shifter? "I-I don't know..."

"Here. Take these." T handed her a pair of oversized, round sunglasses.

Lilliana rolled her eyes. "I'm going for dinner in a restaurant, not hiding from the paparazzi."

Her friend tilted her face forward and lifted an eyebrow. "They're spelled to provide optimal vision performance in dim or bright places. As long as there's some light, you'll be able to see. But no light whatsoever and you're outta luck. They're great to hide behind or provide even more mystery."

They didn't appear to be anything more than a pair of fashion shades. Lilliana slipped them on. Not even a dimming of the light. Huh. She glanced at her appearance. Even more mysterious, not much like sensible accountant Lilliana Vargas at all.

"Where did you get these? My uncle would pay—"

"My dad came up with the spell." T shook her head sharp and quick. "It's a prototype, so I'd appreciate you not letting anyone know."

On second thought, Manny didn't deserve any help whatsoever. "Can do."

T handed her a clutch purse about the size of a thin, hardback book. "Can carry about what your current purse would and turns into a belt bag if you hold it to your waist."

Impressive, since Lilliana squeezed half the world into her tote. "You need to get into the protection business. Men only think of themselves when designing gear."

A sly smile grew across her friend's features. "More on that later, but no telling anyone about these. You've got ten minutes to get to the restaurant."

Bless T for knowing how Lilliana hated being late and it would take nearly the entire ten to get there.

She quickly slipped the amulet she'd "appropriated" from her uncle's desk under her blouse where a ruffle would hide the glimmer. Then she transferred her wallet, phone, and a thumb drive to the purse. "Can I leave this here?" With her friend's outstretched hand, Lilliana handed over her simple leather bag. "How much do I owe you?"

"Nothing." The sorcerer crossed her arms and shot Lilliana a quelling look.

"But—"

"You've been with me through thick and thin. You were my friend even when people called me names for having a mixed magic family, and even despite your own parents' disapproval. You believed in me enough to help fund this store. Did my books that first year. I'm doing really well." T blinked rapidly, then turned toward the back of the shop and started walking away. "It's all on me," she said, her voice drifting over her shoulder. "Now get out of here before you ruin my makeup."

Lilliana tracked her friend until she disappeared into the boutique's back room. She hitched a laugh because her friend had caused mist to form in her own eyes. The sorceress wasn't the only grateful one. She caught a glance of the First Bank of Enchanted Rock's clock hanging in the window across the pedestrian walkway. Yikes. Nine minutes left. No time for dawdling.

Fortunately, the Rock wasn't crowded as she made her way toward the elevators, which would take her to the restaurant on the fringes of Clan Shifter's dedicated area.

If only her thoughts were more like the quiet Sunday evening crowds. Mentally, she ass-kicked herself for not recognizing how easily he could've concluded the bindings might have a backdoor. Then there was the indescribable knowledge she'd met him before that remained stuck in her mind, like gum to her shoe on a hot Texas day.

No matter how much she'd taxed her brain on the hour drive to the Rock, she couldn't figure it out. She'd grown up in Illusion, went to Illusion schools, worked in the Clan Magic accounting department headquartered in Illusion. The only time she'd even socialized with shifters was on a couple of occasions she'd been to Mingo's bar in Enchanted Rock's all-clan common area. Too loud and too many beings.

Maybe he'd taken a new ID potion in the past and this was his real appearance. Or was this his fake appearance?

Ugh. She'd just have to be a better detective, that's all. Not get tongue-tied in his mere presence like she had been in the Santiago Systems showroom. Why hadn't she thought to ask his full name? A shifter named Caleb. Not a lot to go on.

Doubts began to crowd in. She should be at home reviewing the financial accounts her uncle had stored on his computer that she'd downloaded earlier today onto the thumb drive contained in her purse. She was supposed to meet Detective Slocomb in a couple of hours and had been expected to have already completed a preliminary analysis.

A storefront's window reflected her image, and for a moment, she nearly didn't believe the vision was her. More doubts pushed their way into her thoughts until she shoved the mass aside.

She could do this, and her outfit would be her new persona. She'd always been a good actor—was often the lead in her school plays and she had a couple of leading roles in the acting courses she'd taken as electives in college. Besides, if she could fool everyone into thinking she actually cared for Derwin, she could pull this off.

Her grandmother came to mind. Her father's mother was a confident woman of elite Clan Magic society, belonged to the right country club, wore the right clothing, and expected a large amount of respect. Echoes from summers Lilliana spent with her grandmother flooded back. *Stand tall, girl. Stop looking so meek. You're a Vargas. Act like it.*

All Lilliana needed was a little straightening of her shoulders. Not hard because the shoes begged her to stand tall. Maybe she could add a little more purpose to her walk, easy since the shoes seemed to want her to strut herself. The slightest upward tilt to her chin added to her role. Plus, the glasses hid any uncertainty in her eyes.

A tall, attractive male snagged her gaze as he approached her. He gave her the once-over and sharp fangs appeared in his appreciative smile.

Her fingers curled around the clutch, and she shot back what she hoped to be a confident grin, one that said she knew just how hot she was and might—just might, mind you—entertain a flirtation from the demon. With his hesitation, as if he would stop to talk, her self-assurance returned. She continued her long strides, safe once more within the role she'd assumed, not unlike the one she'd taken on during her entire life around her family or the time on Smoke Roundtree's crew. Only this time, she'd jettison the nastiness and got to wear cooler clothing than black tactical gear.

She approached the restaurant and despite the hundred or so yards remaining, she spied the shifter outside, his hands braced on his hips. He spoke with someone, the very large someone from two nights ago, who then pivoted and walked away.

The red-haired hottie turned toward her.

Usually, she wouldn't have ascribed 'hawt' to a man with red hair. This one, though, wore his hair a bit long and pulled back into a small bun at his nape. A bit of scruff on his strong jaw temped her to stroke the rough texture, while his marvelously complex hazel eyes with their jumble of bright green, brown, and copper, made her want to swoon.

"*Swoon?*" Her grandmother's voice screeched in her head. She snapped her spine straight and ignored any idea that the sleekly muscled shifter across from her could be attractive. Even in the crisp, white, silk dress shirt and fine wool slacks, which spoke of money.

She drew up to him, her lips feeling as if they'd been sewn shut. His hair held a bit of dampness. The clean, soapy fragrance still couldn't cover the scent of evergreen and musk… and something wild that called to her like a lover.

Her mouth dried as he continued to hold her gaze. Dammit. She'd blown her role already. Wait a minute. He couldn't see behind the glasses. She could still play the part.

When she shoved one side of her hair over her shoulder, he widened his eyes, and she fought back a little snicker. She's forgotten he'd be able to make out the solid black bra she wore underneath the filmy blouse.

For some reason, his response galvanized her. She slipped off the sunglasses and shot him a smile that said she knew exactly where he'd been staring.

He firmed his jaw, and she was glad he didn't shave the scruff, which added an aura of ruggedness to his red-headed good looks. "I didn't think you'd show."

"Don't know why." She dropped her chin a little and shot him a mocking glance. "Shall we eat?"

7

Caleb's gaze seemed glued to Lilliana's ass while she followed the maître d' to their table.

The idea to meet her here was to satisfy two needs, food and confirmation of how she'd defeated the Santiago Systems security features. Now he'd added another need.

Her.

His wolf howled in approval. For the love of...

Had this been a tactical mistake? Because right now it was all he could do to keep his canine alter ego from taking over and dragging her to his quarters for a night of hot, sweaty sex.

Figured his animalistic side would completely ignore the enigma that was Lilliana Vargas. Before he'd showered and changed, he'd called Cheese and asked for a full workup on the mage.

"Why?" Bright interest had popped into Cheese's tone. Of course she'd be interested in Lilliana after she'd somehow escaped the NACS roundup of Smoke Roundtree's crew. Especially when she'd fried Caleb's ass. Cheese was vindictive like that.

He'd debated on whether to tell the analyst, then hedged, saying he thought he might have a line on her again. He'd also omitted the fact he knew the mage's identity during his interviews with the various law enforcement agencies and still couldn't understand his compulsion.

For this meeting, he'd dressed in a fresh shirt and slacks, then added his nicest belt and roper-style boots. While he'd like to believe he cleaned up because The Werehouse had a dress code, his wolf merely huffed a laugh. The Coffeys decided their own dress code, and no one had the balls to deny them service.

The background had come back from Cheese about ten minutes before he was supposed to meet Lilliana. Nothing much, except she had taken a leave of absence from her job with Clan Magic in their accounting department. No criminal history. Nothing which indicated she'd hang out with known jewel thieves—well, reformed jewel thieves—like Smoke Roundtree.

Zero out of the ordinary, but one fact glared. She'd been working at Santiago Systems, something the report didn't mention. Why would she need to do that? Gambling debts? Magical drug addiction? Or just wanted to supplement her government check to afford the luxuries she'd undoubtedly gotten used to while growing up? Before she'd hung up, Cheese said she'd look into the matter and get back with him.

Lilliana slid into a booth's seat, which pulled him from his thoughts and his contemplation of the mysterious woman's fine ass. The maître d's gaze lingered on her body. The slightest hint of unreasonable pride sparked to life, and Caleb quickly banished the idea. She wasn't his, and she only came here to protect her secret.

He slid into the other end of the round booth, its sides high and padded in diamond-tufted, supple leather. After the maître d' distributed the menus and wine list, he quirked an eyebrow to Caleb, who returned a short nod to indicate the booth met with his approval.

The male retreated, and Caleb swung his gaze to the enigmatic mage. Lilliana finished placing her sunglasses in her purse, then set the small black bag on the table. With a graceful flick of her wrist, she shook out the napkin's complex fold and placed the dark fabric on her lap.

She swept her gaze up to meet his with a small, tight tilt to her lips. "Now then, before we start, I would like to know your name. You know mine. It's only fair to know yours."

"You don't remember nearly frying my ass?" almost tumbled from his lips before he clamped his mouth shut. He searched her for any signs of deception but found none. He'd been in shifted form then, so possibly she told the truth.

"Caleb Coffey."

"Okay, Caleb." She laced her fingers together, and her skin appeared fine and pale against the dark table linen. "I'd prefer not to discuss business until after the meal. I didn't have time today to eat lunch, and I would very much like the small ribeye, a loaded baked potato, and some broccoli."

He suppressed a chuckle at her attempt to control the meeting. She could…for a time. "Very well."

Luckily, the server stopped to bring water at that moment. Caleb repeated her order, then added his own, the double-cut prime rib, no sides. Could he have ordered the quadruple-sized? The rumbling coming from his stomach said "absolutely." But instinct told him she'd try to make this brief, and he wasn't going to waste food if he didn't have to. Along with the massive cut of beef, he added a bottle of cabernet. A case of wine chugged one bottle after the other might accomplish inebriation in a shifter, so he didn't worry about the alcohol.

He caught her raised eyebrows. Perhaps he should've consulted her first. "My manners are appalling enough you'd think I was raised in a pigsty. You okay with red? You can have whatever you'd prefer."

"Cabernet's fine." She hesitated for a moment, then asked, "If you weren't raised in a sty, where *did* you grow up?"

On its face, the question seemed innocuous enough, possibly two people getting to know each other better. Her swift, keen glance quickly shuttered, suggesting there was more than casual interest to her inquiry.

"I grew up in Asheville, North Carolina. I have two siblings, one a veterinarian, the other in finance, like my father." He held her gaze during the recitation. "I'm 54 years old and I'm single. Spent a bit of time with Clan Shifter Security. I now work for a private investigation company, but you probably already know that."

Greek he could read. Her features, however, were as unreadable to him as the Mayan language. He lifted his water glass from the dark tablecloth and took a sip. After he swallowed and she hadn't yet replied, he asked, "And you?"

She shot a glance to her clutch, then back to him. The wine steward arrived at that moment, interrupting any reply she might've made. Once the opening ritual had been completed, the starchily-attired male poured the two glasses and then retreated, and Caleb focused on Lilliana once more. Not that he didn't know her background, courtesy of Cheese, but would she lie?

"Lilliana Vargas. Forty-two. I grew up in Illusion and work as an accountant for Clan Magic."

He stared at her for a moment, but when her chin tilted up, he added to her resume, "And Santiago Systems."

She snatched her wine glass from the table and took a hefty swig. If he was a betting wolf, he'd say she was either coming up with a lie or trying to figure out how much truth to tell him.

She swallowed, then twirled the stem a bit with her fingers. "My uncle has had some turnover lately, and I said I would help for a couple of weeks." She took another sip, this time more delicately, and carefully replaced the glass, pushing the stemware back into place with the tips of her fingers.

While Caleb believed she told the truth, the short response begged more questions than it answered. But he let it go for now—her salad had arrived. He kept his counsel while she studiously finished the greens and studied her instead.

Or, more accurately, the contrast of her. Two days ago, she'd been confident and full of purpose. Maybe not knowledgeable about tactical situations, but certainly a fast learner and sharp. Earlier today, though, she'd appeared unsure, perhaps even panicked, when he talked about going to her uncle. And now...

The beautiful stranger across from him laid her fork at the correct angle on the plate. If there was one thing he knew, it was manners. His parents drummed enough of those elitist rules in him so he wouldn't embarrass their high-dollar friends. According to Cheese's profile, her parents were physicians, and one spell her father had both developed and patented made the family a second fortune atop the one initially made by his mother and her legal practice.

A server appeared table side and whisked away her salad plate. In its place, he set her entree, then Caleb's. Once he'd departed, Caleb planned to return to his subtle—or possibly not-so-subtle—interrogation.

First, he cut a nice, thick piece of ribeye and mopped the chunk in some of the juices. The bite satisfied his tastebuds but not his stomach, which begged for more once he'd swallowed the mouthful. Before satiating his gut, he should ask another question. "How did you end up in accounting?"

She had just dipped her fork into her potato. For a moment, he thought she might not answer, then her lips curved without humor. "You mean, how did I end up in the Accounting Department at Clan Magic making government wages when I could've probably landed a job with First Bank of Enchanted Rock since my father sits on the board?"

Whoa. Her acid tone cut to the bone. "I didn't have time to do a deep dive into the background on you that Cheese gave me, but—"

Her eyes bugged and she swallowed, then started coughing violently.

Prepared to jump into abdominal thrust action, he put his fork down. "You okay?"

Face red, eyes watering, she used her hand to wave him off while she finished clearing her airway from behind her napkin.

He popped in another piece of steak while he kept careful watch. Though he wouldn't mind his arms around her, he didn't want the purpose to be for removing a choking hazard.

Lilliana took a couple of drafts from her water glass. "You said 'Cheese.' As in Brianne Collins? You work for Hebert Security? Geezus." She sat back against the seat, covered her eyes with one hand, and began mumbling to herself.

He thought he heard "dumbass" a couple of times, but her muted ranting was largely unintelligible. Fascinating.

Finally she heaved a deep breath and dropped her hand. "You're Uno."

The accusation in her glare caught him unaware. "Yes?"

She grabbed her knife and fork and attacked the steak with a vengeance, then shoved a bite into her mouth. Around her chew, she said, "You could've told me." She ate another big bite of meat and began to chew.

"You didn't ask."

A chiming came from her right, and she grabbed her purse with jerky movements. She removed her phone and stared at the screen for several more rings.

"You going to answer that?"

She didn't reply, but swallowed, then stabbed her finger on the screen. For several moments, she held the device to her ear. She paled and began to nibble on her lower lip. Finally, she said, "Yes, I can. I'm ready now. Send me the information."

Intriguing. Sounded like some sort of meet.

She returned the device to her purse and sat back. While her eyes were aimed in his direction, by the thousand-yard stare, he'd bet she didn't really see him. She shook her head lightly, like she'd cleared her thoughts, then gazed down at her plate with longing before glancing back to him. "I've got to go."

Both he and his wolf came to attention. "Not yet. You haven't answered my questions."

"I'll answer them the next time I see you."

Though he didn't intend on allowing her to leave, the pleasure socking him in the solar plexus that she might want to see him again caught him unaware. "When will that be?"

"We'll find a time." She tossed her napkin on the table, then picked up her purse and took one scoot toward the banquet's edge. "Look, I may not be able to answer your questions, but I'll try, okay? I owe you at least that much for nearly cooking you in Cheese's cabin. But now I have to leave."

An apology? He'd need more than that from her. His phone began to ring, the tone he'd programmed in for his boss. Caleb ignored the notification and pushed himself toward the seat's edge. "Don't you go—"

She opened a personal portal, stepped through, and closed the oval behind her.

8

Lilliana removed the sunglasses from her purse and shoved them on. If she had to go to the Underground's auction, at least she'd already dressed like a confident woman, and the shades would help hide her identity even more. Now that she knew Derwin was involved, she'd have to be on the tips of her toes. Luckily, the clothing, hair, and glasses would make a decent cover. Her look was definitely not the normal Lilliana Vargas.

After she put on her shades, she extracted her phone from the clutch as well. Detective Meadows sent the electronic invitation to the device, as well as the vortex ticket to Sedona, typically a popular destination and sold out at least a week in advance. He even provided a VIP pass so she wouldn't have to wait on standby for someone not to show.

She entered the velvet-roped line, which had no one waiting. Once she provided her confirmation number, the agent told her the departure was on time. Great. Eight minutes to go.

An empty seat to the side beckoned, and she settled into the padding. Lilliana would've preferred to not have even that short time to think about who Caleb was and why the wolf set every fiber of her being aflame.

Kind of like you nearly set him on fire?

Damn her nerves. She'd done better at the Underground holding site two nights ago. The more confidence she had, the easier time she had casting spells. Several weeks ago, she'd been nervy and uncertain if she was handling her role properly, and her lack of confidence showed. Her immobility spell had gone wonky, and she almost lost it when the smell of singed fur hit her nose. She might as well have been a mage in training once more.

Until she came face to face with Caleb in the restaurant, she'd nearly been able to banish the embarrassing moment from her memory. He would certainly rebuff any advance she made, even if she got up enough courage to act on her unreasonable desires.

"Sedona Vortex travelers, please line up," a smooth voice announced over the speaker.

Lilliana rose and joined the couple of beings in the VIP line, one much shorter than those who paid for regular fare. She covertly studied the three males and one female in the queue with her. Two of the males carried backpacks and wore clothing she associated with outdoor activities—shirts and pants of technical fabric with hiking boots. If she had to guess, they were either Clan Human Paranormal or Clan Magic.

By the way the female clung to the last male, the two traveled together. A short smile revealed his fangs, while an answering grin showed she had none. His dress, slightly European with its dark slacks, shirt, and blazer, would lead Lilliana to bet her last dime he was a demon, and the female was most likely his HP blood concubine.

Lilliana shuddered a bit at the idea of someone drinking her blood for sustenance.

A small, snarky voice chimed in, *Not that different from eating a rare steak.*

But at least I'm not getting sexual gratification while I feed as well.

The willowy, uniformed attendant approached the cordon. By her light coloration and lithe form, probably a fae. Maybe not an elf, though, since most wouldn't debase themselves with this low a job. She lifted the hook from the stanchion pole and used a sweep of her arm with the barest hint of a polite smile to indicate the VIP travelers could proceed. "Keep moving please," was her only instruction.

"Easy peasy, lemon squeezy," as Thelma would say. When Lilliana approached the large, swirling silver disc, a small commotion behind her would've had her pause. But by her stopping, the line might bottleneck, so she continued.

She stepped through the vortex from the pink-granite-walled Enchanted Rock and into the red-granite-walled Sedona Vortex with the only sensation being the raised hair on her arms and the back of her neck, like she'd encountered a static charge. Others said the travel made them queasy or knocked them out.

Vargases are made of sterner stuff, her grandmother's voice added with a disdainful sniff.

Lilliana continued walking into the reception area so she didn't hinder anyone traveling behind her. Besides, if she stopped moving, her knees would probably start shaking. She scanned the signs held by several people in simple black suits. One of the chauffeurs had the alias last name the detective provided.

Stenson. First name, Carmen, if anyone needed to know.

But they wouldn't need the given name with the code she'd been sent. The same code would allow her to bid on the women to be sold.

Like Anna.

Lilliana wanted to believe she could be her cousin's savior, and her mouth dried with the uncertainty of what she would face.

She exited with the driver and climbed into the back of the luxury SUV. A bottle of water sat in a cupholder, and she greedily downed the entirety, grimacing when she still wanted more.

Instead of opening another bottle, she reviewed the short conversation with the detective. He'd said Anna had been listed as one for sale, and he couldn't have a team there, though he did have someone on the inside. She should look for a thin male with snow-white hair named Barry. He would accept the thumb drive as well.

Those were the orders, and she rolled them over and over to avoid contemplating Caleb. She needed to focus on her mission —Rescue her cousin and deliver the thumb drive to Barry. The small bits of salad and two bites of steak sloshed in her stomach, making her wish she hadn't gulped the water.

In what seemed like no time at all, the SUV drove up to a set of ornate metal gates. The chauffeur punched a code into a keypad. A sense of unease rippled through her as the massive panels swung open. This wasn't a luxury rideshare, but one provided by the Underground.

Worry for her cousin circled constantly in her mind, and she prayed she'd be in time. Tremors threatened to erupt in her fingers, and she clasped them tight, grateful for the cover provided by the sunglasses. At least no one would be able to see her eyes—and half her face—with them on. Plus, like Thelma promised, everything in the SUV's interior was clearly visible, as if in daylight.

While the driver continued through the gates toward a moodily lit, two-story, adobe mansion, Lilliana's tension increased with each second until her shoulders were so stiff she thought she might snap in two.

Relax. She rolled down the window to allow any fear pheromones she might've released to escape the interior. The Underground employed shifters, and she didn't need them picking up on her nerves. She wanted to not just rescue her cousin but also to stay alive.

The window's air tugged at several strands of her hair, and she tucked them behind her ear. *Don't think. Enjoy the moment.* The breeze's warm fingers played over her face. In her imagination Caleb's fingers ruffled the edges of her lace blouse.

Ahead loomed the mansion. She halted the thought and rolled up her window. She needed to stay focused because she'd be getting out in a couple of seconds anyway. *Remember your role.* Only a confident woman could possibly move in the Underground circles. Something hovered at the edge of her mind, but she brushed aside the worry. No time for more doubts now. With a tilt of her chin and a straightening of her spine, she once again donned the persona of a wealthy woman unconcerned with anything other than herself.

You can do this. Keep your eyes open, your thoughts guarded from a telepath, and an immobilization spell at the ready.

The quick pep talk buoyed her flagging confidence just in time. The SUV came to a gentle halt and a massive male garbed in a tuxedo opened the door for her to exit.

She didn't hesitate but slid from the vehicle's leather seat and stalked toward the gigantic wooden double doors without a backward glance. Ordinarily, she would've thanked the driver and the attendant. But in this world of the criminally wealthy, she couldn't afford to make mistakes. Here, just like in her grandmother's sphere, little people deserved no notice, let alone courtesy.

At the door, two beings stood, one tall and muscled, the other shorter than Lilliana and almost as round. His sharp, pointed face suggested gremlin.

The tall one swept her from head to toe, while the short one held out what appeared to be some sort of scanner. "Credentials, please."

She unlocked her phone and displayed the QR code she'd been provided. Hopefully, the ennui she'd pasted on her features held while she took in as much of her surroundings as she could. No visible cameras. There must be some. The Underground would certainly use someone's participation in this illegal activity against them if able.

The scanner's green light and beep made her want to cheer and pump her fist, but she carefully released the air from her lungs. When the gargoyle swept his hand to the heavy, iron-studded doors, she strode through head held high.

When she crossed the threshold, the ear-popping experience of crossing an active ward almost made her stop, but she continued without hesitation. The barrier hadn't been set to repel, so that left two options—keep people in or stop them from using any sort of paranormal gift. Maybe both. Apprehension reared, but somehow she kept moving.

Inside, a woman in a slinky black dress waited, her expression so blank she might've been taken for a robot. "Please continue down the hallway, then to the right."

"There you are."

Lilliana froze. Surely that wasn't...

Stay in character!

She released the tension gripping her shoulders and turned languidly, shifting hair over her shoulder with a negligent hand. Hopefully the robotic attendant couldn't hear her pounding pulse.

Caleb paced toward her. But somehow not Caleb. While the shifter she'd left at the restaurant carried an aura of danger, he'd added power and great fortune to his demeanor. His gaze raked her possessively, like a meal he intended to devour.

A shiver traveled down her spine. He had on the same clothing, wore the same custom, smooth Ostrich boots. Who was this wolf, really? Why was he here? Bees started buzzing in her stomach, churning her meager dinner to vaguely nauseating.

He stopped in front of her, forcing her to tip her head back until she met his glittering gaze. Was that a hint of "play along," or was he trying to communicate something more sinister?

You bought this farm. Till the fields. Buck up. Be witty. "I wasn't lost," she said with a crisp note of surly dryness.

Instead of responding to her comment, he presented an arm. "Walk with me."

She had no other play at this moment than to thread her arm through his and begin their stroll down the broad hallway. His warmth radiated through his shirt's fine silk, and she shivered, wishing she could soak up more. Though her brain distantly registered the artwork she passed—Picasso, Monet, Mondrian, Hans the Younger—her mind reeled.

Focus! Without knowing how to find her cousin prior to the auction, Lilliana needed to stay on her toes.

A large, gilt-framed sign sat on a brass easel ahead. At the top it read, "Auctions Begin at Ten Thousand Fae Gold Coins" in elegant script, with a slightly smaller subheading, "Bidding Begins promptly at 6:00 p.m." A list of specialized paranormal talents underneath ran the gamut of clans. “Telekinetics.” “Dragon shifter.” “Gargoyle.” “Level One Mage.” “Elf.” Nowhere on the placard was “Witch.” Why had they taken Anna? Unless she failed to declare something more special to the clan’s registry department, Lilliana, as a Level One mage, especially one who could travel farther via portal than most mages, would’ve been a far better target...

Her gaze zeroed in on “Level One Mage.” Fear prickled along her nape, and her pulse skipped. What had been lurking at the fringes of her logic burst forward like a childhood “I told you so.” Would a female even be welcome at one of these auctions where misogyny ruled?

Her stomach began to roil. She reviewed the call from the detective. A contact where she was supposed to drop off the only evidence she had and somehow rescue her cousin? Otherwise, she’d have no support. When she got the call, she’d been filled with panic and jumped at the chance of the last possibility to save Anna. Just like the last minute call to the Elgin warehouse.

Instead, her rescue had become a suicide mission rife with the possibility Lilliana been the target all along.

9

LILLIANA'S FEAR spiked in Caleb's nose, and he stopped, forcing her to halt as well. He shifted his hands to curl his fingers around her hips, then tugged gently toward the shadows at the side of the wide, moodily lit foyer.

"Calm down," he murmured.

This was the role he knew he couldn't fuck up. He morphed his expression to hint tenderness, then tucked a strand of hair behind her ear. A lover's caress. He bent to whisper, "You're throwing off fear like a baby deer in a wolf's sights."

She placed her palms on his chest, wiggled her fingers slightly, then tilted her head back offering him a sultry pout on her lips. "I just cast a silence spell. Are you the big bad wolf, or one who will get me out of the mess I think I just put myself in?"

His feral side howled with approval. "You can trust me. Detective Slocomb is actually an Underground mole in Clan Magic Security. NACS is trying to get a team assembled, but we'll be on our own for a while. Just stick with me, okay?"

Goose bumps broke out over the skin of her upper arms, and she paled.

Did he blame her? No, but every second she delayed was one less second for escape.

She wound her arms around his neck, then murmured into his ear, "Thank you for saving me from my own stupidity."

The soft crush of her breasts against his chest and her warm breath caused sensations to cascade through him, bringing his wolf to whine for more. No time for the beast right now. He turned to the front door to see if that might be a way to escape.

His gaze landed on an approaching male. Dammit. He knew this asshole, a shifter associate of his father's, though he couldn't remember his name. General knowledge of Caleb's line of work probably wouldn't cause a problem, since his father only ever told his acquaintances that Caleb was "off enjoying himself and would join the family bank in a few years." Yet, best to try to avoid this shifter if possible.

He placed his hands on Lilliana's waist, picked her up, then deposited her between the wall and his body. Manhandling women wouldn't be out of character here.

Though her mouth formed a little "O", mercifully, she played along with him, licking her lips, then catching one between her teeth. In all, a good job of pretending the press of his body aroused her.

"Going to kiss you now."

He didn't give her time to say no. Hopefully, the other wolf wouldn't notice Caleb's hair, the same color as his father's and quite distinctive.

Without any preamble, he brought his lips to hers. He sank into her wet heat, and his tongue swept in, seeking, like this wasn't the first time they'd kissed.

A low moan came from her with a softening of her body as

she melded with him. Her fingers both clutched at his nape and pressure built at his ass, where her other hand urged him impossibly closer. His wolf reveled in her softness, how her body moved against him, then found all the right places to fit together.

The scent of her arousal filled his nose, and he wanted nothing more than to taste her wet heat.

"Caleb? Caleb Coffey?"

Distantly, he heard the male. How had she pulled him under so quickly? He paused to compose himself. The mission was to rescue Lilliana, not to make love to her.

He turned, ensuring to keep her behind him, and pasted on what he called his thin, country-club smile. With little other option, he shook the proffered hand. "Been a while."

The male nodded his head. "I'm glad the Coffeys have finally gotten with the program. I've been telling your father for some time he should take advantage of what the Underground can provide." The male's gaze flicked slightly to the side, then back to Caleb. "Like that little filly you've got right there."

The smug way he spoke about a group of criminals who abused females set Caleb's blood on fire. Then when the asshole referred to Lilliana... Lucky for him that the Underground employed wards to keep paranormals from using their abilities. Otherwise, Caleb would've shifted and torn the wolf in front of him to pieces.

His father's associate emitted an uneasy chuckle and held up his hands palms out. "My apologies. I can see she must be new if you're that into her."

Caleb forced his growling wolf back but didn't bother to restrain the alpha vibes. He stared at the man until the male took a step back and broke eye contact.

"Excuse me, sir."

The words came from his left. For several more moments, Caleb stared the other wolf into submission, then turned to the beautiful automaton who'd greeted him at the door. "What?"

The sharpness he'd added to the word didn't appear to faze the female. "My lord has rooms available for his guests should they need them."

Behind him, Lilliana cut off a short, sharp inhale.

The asshole across from him slid away without further comment.

A room might just be what he needed—get Lilliana out of sight. He forced his features into a superior mask. "Which way might those be?"

"Bear left at the end of the hallway, then take the stairs to the second floor. An attendant will direct you further." Her vapid smile matched the rote cadence. They must have spelled her to behave in this manner. Anger bit at his gut.

Didn't matter because he needed to get Lilliana up those stairs and out of sight. Now.

He pivoted slightly, then extended his hand, gratified when she accepted his lead. He used his peripheral vision to surveil his surroundings on the way to the staircase. No guards flanked the doors to other rooms, suggesting they would let the wards do their job. The controls not only ensured their captives couldn't use special abilities to escape, but also ensured the "guests" played nice. When you had the likes of Griffith Jenkins and members of the Sunda Crime Syndicate typically in attendance, the situation could get dicey.

She walked with him and didn't buck the arm he crossed around her back, ending with his hand on her hip. When he pulled her close, she pressed the heavy weight of his gun in its hidden waistband holster against him. He'd strapped his fae silver knife against his calf, and its weight gave him comfort.

Few preferred knives anymore, believing guns were the most efficient weapon. His knife, though, would slice through everything except dragon scale, while spelled bullets would only incapacitate. With any luck, he could get her out of this potential kidnapping trap.

Though he'd been stripped of the power to shift—hence the gun—his hearing, sight, and sense of smell still functioned. He opened them to their fullest ability, catalogued Lilliana's heartbeats, then pushed them to the background in favor of searching for other sounds.

Hopefully, his haste would be attributed to lovers wanting to fuck. Part of him regretted this would not be what happened in the room. Assuming he got her that far.

An attendant waited at the top of the stairs. Whiffs of warm rock gave away the large fae as a gargoyle, just like the one who'd manned the front door with the gremlin. Discerning one paranormal from another could be difficult, but Caleb's nose learned the essential scents of almost all beings, though they could be covered with some sort of potion or spell.

The attendant—more a guard, really—swept his gaze over him and Lilliana, a slight lift to his upper lip. "Room, sir?"

"Yes."

"Bidding begins in forty-five minutes, and all guests are required to attend." His hard stare suggested he'd personally haul Caleb and Lilliana from whatever carnal act if necessary. "Third door on your left, please, sir."

Caleb snuck a quick glance to Lilliana, who he'd tucked against his side.

While her fingers gripped his waist, her back remained straight, and her head still tilted in a regal way. Her demeanor said she didn't care what the smirking gargoyle might think, though behind the glasses, who could tell? Smart to use them as a shield, even if they'd limit her ability to see in a lower light.

He gently squeezed his fingers where they sat at the upper curve of her hip, trying to communicate "not long now."

Only about sixty feet remained to possible freedom. He forced himself to cross the distance in a leisurely fashion, even slid his hand to her ass.

A strangled sound squeaked from her, one she tried to cover with a throaty chuckle. "Darling, not in front of the staff. You can wait one more minute."

"You know you're irresistible." He'd added a faint growl to his tone.

Her hand curled under the knot he pulled his hair into at his nape, and the slight scratch of her nails against his scalp set his skin to tingling.

Damn. She really knew how to make his blood sing. He fumbled with the handle of the door the gargoyle had indicated, then swept her inside, shutting the thick wood panel behind him. A deadbolt lock sat underneath the knob inside. He used his thumb to turn the latch, which probably would only stop someone from accidentally entering.

Cameras or two-way mirrors or even microphones could be hidden in the room, and he scanned the interior. The luxury desert theme continued here as well, with a curved, adobe fireplace in the corner along the outside wall and dark beams overhead. The king-sized bed was draped in a sandy silk coverlet, which matched the muted tones in the rest of the sumptuous furnishings. The Underground always rented their auction venues. The changing locations frustrated law enforcement's efforts to halt their unconscionable activity. This was most likely a rent-a-mansion, one on an exclusive list for the superrich. Nothing Caleb hadn't seen before.

More importantly, a set of double doors sat directly ahead. Possible escape route one. An open doorway on the opposite wall from the bed suggested a bathroom. If it had a window, possible escape route two. Hopefully, they hadn't been spelled or warded or whatever magic was used for protection.

He tugged on her hip to pull her against him and met her questioning gaze, though she remained silent. Smart as a whip, this one. She'd guessed the room might be monitored. He dipped his head until his lips met hers.

This time, he prepared for the surge of heat threatening to swamp him. When she moaned, he forced himself to stay above his need to sweep her into his arms, lay her on the bed and sample every inch of skin, every hollow, so he could once more savor the scent of her arousal into his lungs. Even his wolf growled at the whisper of those desires drifting through his mind.

Safety first, sex later. He treated this moment no differently than when he would compartmentalize the pain of a spelled bullet. He could continue his actions while shuttling the feeling into another portion of his mind.

He shifted positions to face the bathroom door and trailed his lips to her ear. "Go with me," he said on a bare whisper while he nuzzled the delicate shell.

One of her hands had wandered to his ass, and she squeezed a bit to acknowledge his words. His moan was genuine. With his mouth still slanting against hers, he moved several steps forward.

She went with him until her back met the wall. He glanced inside. Damn. No window, but there was a slice he couldn't see.

Again he moved his mouth to her ear. "Can you see an escape route?"

She arched her neck, and he obediently trailed his lips

down her soft skin to where her pulse beat wildly. Though he knew he shouldn't, he sucked lightly.

"Oh, *yes*," she said on a gasp.

The heavy emphasis on the last word told him a second option existed. The breathlessness with which she delivered the short phrase also told him he should stop teasing her. Her scent, the one his wolf wanted to roll in and mark as his own, rose once more to his nose.

He stilled. *Oh no.*

His wolf nodded. *Mine.*

Not now. Not like this. He pushed the idea Lilliana might be his mate to the side and doubled down on his concentration. If the room was monitored, they'd observe any escape attempts. And, if they were truly planning to take Lilliana like he suspected, they would know she was nice and tight right here. Best get to getting.

Heavy footfalls sounded outside the room, ending with a sharp knock.

They'd reacted faster than he expected. With a sharpening of his senses, he met her gaze, a small part of him satisfied her face was flushed and her lips were swollen from his kisses. "We're going to have to fight our way out."

"I can help." She raced toward the set of double doors.

He wanted to tell her not when the organization dampened critical paranormal powers. But she'd been resourceful. Maybe she had something that would help. To buy time, he said with his most irritated tone, "What?'

"You must open the door, or we will come in." The bellowed words seemed to be from the lump of granite in charge of the room assignments.

She circled her hand to tell him to keep delaying, then slapped the purse to her side, where it transformed into a smaller rectangle and stuck. Neat trick. Clan Magic got all the nice stuff. Perhaps the rooms hadn't been warded like the rest of the house.

"Just a moment," he said, then added a string of expletives to indicate he was not pleased at being interrupted.

She smacked her hand against the center of the French doors. Sparks whistled and buzzed under her palm.

A heavy thump sounded against the hallway door, and it bowed. The voice bellowed, "Kick it down."

"Come on." Lilliana's urgent whisper turned him from attempting to brace the door to racing toward her. Duh. She'd counteracted the ward at the warehouse a couple of days ago. Dammit. He should've guessed she had an ability to work with this one as well. That's how she worked her silence spell earlier. He castigated himself for being such a dumbass for not recognizing she'd used her magic in the silencing spell, which the Underground's protections should've prevented. And if Santiago Systems was involved with this syndicate, they must've set these wards too.

The thud of something hitting the door behind him came immediately before the wood's *crack*. He reached the balcony. Since the house faced a downslope and appeared to allow for a full story below where he entered, the jump would be about forty feet. He could withstand the impact, but how could she?

"Halt," a male voice ordered from behind him.

No fucking way.

Caleb glanced at her, and she nodded. At the same time as she, he vaulted over the railing.

10

LILLIANA CALLED a spell to buoy her descent. The short distance didn't allow for much time to decelerate, but damn if the high-heeled sandals didn't soften the blow when she landed.

Once she straightened, she turned to Caleb, who had already drawn his gun. Oh, to be as swift as a shifter.

He grabbed her hand and tugged her around the edge of the large pool toward a pathway. The shoes weren't bad to run in, but on the packed earth pathway, she wished she had the time to change them into the sneakers. At least the narrow lane was lined with low lighting. Plus, her "sunglasses" provided her vision as clear as if the sun were shining. Excitement that she'd escaped the mansion warred with the desperation to elude the Underground's henchmen.

She tried to keep up, but knew she slowed him down.

A spell came whizzing by, exploding into a cactus that burst into flame. She jumped away, then threw a panicked glance over her shoulder.

Derwin led several others in pursuit. Dammit. They were

gaining. And that dark shape above was probably a gargoyle. She slung two quick immobility spells, not surprised she missed with both of them. To be fair, while running, her typically bad aim turned abysmal. She threw two more, hoping for better contact, but all she managed was to slow herself more.

Frustrated by her incompetence, she turned back and found Caleb had shifted into a massive red wolf, easily slipping his back paws from the boots, but pieces of his clothing remained. Along with the gun a few feet away, a knife in a holster lay next to his ropers, something he must've strapped to his calf. He pivoted in a blink and started back toward the beings chasing them.

Heart pounding hard against her ribs, she grabbed the gun and the knife with shaky hands, then took cover behind a large cactus. She lobbed several more spells, but managed to not hit a soul. A gun would be more effective. She glanced down to the hand that held Caleb's weapons. Duh.

Quickly, she tucked the knife into the purse at her waist, chiding herself for being so slow. Her poor processing time could cost Caleb his life.

With a quick peek around the cactus, she spied him dodging a spell and lunging toward Derwin. Somehow, the mage managed to evade the wolf's snapping jaws.

Her peripheral vision caught on a dark blur headed directly toward her shifter. She aimed and pulled the trigger twice. A gargoyle plummeted to earth.

Yes!

She *whooped* with satisfaction, but there was little time for celebration. Behind where the wolf and Derwin were involved in their deadly dance, more people streamed from the back of the mansion. She aimed at several more targets and gloried when the bad guys intending to attack Caleb hit the dirt. She may not be able to throw, but her aim with a gun was true.

Too soon the slide locked back. She had no more bullets. Fear slammed into her sternum. What now?

Duh—portal, you dummy!

She shoved the gun into her purse and dredged as much magical energy as she dared to conjure a portal, one back to a side hallway she'd spied in the Sedona vortex, since it was the only place she knew within a twenty-mile radius. "Caleb, come on!"

He became a virtual blur while he ran to her. What was he doing? He didn't reduce his speed at all.

Time slowed to a frame-by-frame sequence.

Caleb leaped and landed with his front paws on her chest. She fell backward toward the portal and her glasses flew off. He was trying to protect her and would stay behind to fight.

No—he has to come with me.

She managed to grab his front paw and hang on with all her might while she fell. Facing that dangerous crowd could mean his death, no matter what shifter skills he possessed.

Once his back paw was through the oval, she yanked the portal closed, but not before she had a glimpse of a gargoyle swooping in at a trajectory to have landed right where she'd stood.

From the corner of her eye, the red granite floor loomed. She would land partially on her shoulder. Oh, hell. This was going to hurt with the large wolf landing atop her. She squeezed her eyes shut in anticipation.

Time resumed its normal speed.

The landing jarred her entire body. But the expected whack of her head against the hard rock never came. Instead, she landed face down in a heap of fur, muscle, and bone. Her yelp blended with a wolf's grunt.

For a moment she lay there, stunned, heart hammering, lungs fighting for air, while his soft fur tickled her nose, but then the wolf stirred. She stifled a groan and rolled off Caleb and onto the cold, hard granite floor. Between her fright, the effort to conjure the portal, and her self-castigation for nearly getting Caleb killed, she couldn't get up quite yet.

From the corner of her eye, he rose in a halting motion, made all the more strange by the fact he still had on a dress shirt and pants, which hung in places where they'd torn to accommodate his shifted form.

He stared at her with his whiskey-colored eyes, then of all things, he smiled. Well, as much as a wolf could. Then he shook hard, starting at his head, rippling down to his thick tail. In a morphing of muscle and bone, he resumed his two-legged human shape in a matter of moments.

"Sorry you had to see that." His ruined pants began to slide, and he snatched at his waistband with a rueful grin.

She'd been staring up at him like a love-struck teen. Good grief. She dropped her gaze from his handsome face to his sculpted chest revealed by the remaining silk shreds. "No. I've never seen anyone shift. It was so fast, it was a blur. Kind of fascinating. I wonder how it would feel to change shape like that. I mean I can do magic and everything..."

Was she babbling? Why not? He was so gorgeous and tough, not at all like the men she'd dated in the past. He was... yummy. She forced her eyes down his body, his tight abs, the ones she felt when he held her in that awful mansion, slipping past his groin, because she'd just turn into a puddle of goo, down his heavy thighs, and on to his naked feet. How could feet be beautiful? She brought her hand to her temple to make sure she hadn't banged her head on the stone.

He knelt, his gaze scanning her. "Everything okay?" he asked, while he gently ran his large hands over her arms, then legs.

She shivered, wishing for more time when his hands were less clinical and a reserve of power. Traveling this far with another seriously depleted her energy, both magical and physical. Though Derwin couldn't track her precise location, best to get out of Sedona soon.

"I'm fine." Her throat tightened, and she pushed herself to sitting before she made a complete fool of herself by slinging her arms around his neck and pulling him down for a kiss. No matter how exhausted, her desire for this wolf didn't seem to abate. She swallowed to try to clear the dryness in her mouth. "I, uh... Thanks for getting me out of there."

With what seemed almost like reverence, he brought his hand to her cheek, and his gentle smile nearly undid her resolve. "I wasn't going to let anything happen to you. Besides, you did most of the work getting us here."

After a lick to her arid lips, she swallowed again. "I don't know how you did it, but thanks, too, for somehow landing under me so I didn't hit hard."

He tore his focus from her lips and locked his gaze with hers. "You can land on top of me anytime."

The rumbling depth of his low tone set her lady bits to quivering.

He cupped her cheek with his palm and leaned toward her.

Anticipation thumping through her veins, she stretched her neck to meet him halfway, yearning for the lips she'd tasted minutes ago. Just like last time, he took her mouth with a swift, hard passion that melted her insides and sent her head spinning.

Using the scraps of his shirt's soft fabric fisted in her hands, she tugged him closer until he almost tumbled onto her. He chuckled into her mouth and changed the slant of his head. "One more kiss—we need to get moving." He brought one hand to her nape and began a light, stroking rhythm, which sent shivers of desire down her spine, while the other supported her lower back.

She tugged harder, greedy for that single kiss, despite his warning and the disappointment their connection couldn't go further. The granite could be a feather bed for all she cared. She wanted Caleb now. Here.

"Really, Lilliana. A shifter? And in public? Your grandmother would be so disappointed."

She froze. Derwin. His tone scratched like nails against a chalkboard. She leaned back fractionally from Caleb, whose eyes glittered dangerously.

The desire to kill her ex squeezed her gut, and she wished she had more magical energy within her than the paltry amount remaining. She'd need to save her reserves for the right moment. Through tight lips she mouthed, "Derwin Stanford. Mage."

After nodding almost imperceptibly, Caleb rose slowly, then pivoted to face her ex-fiancé. Slim and with a snarky twist to his features, the magic wielder held glowing spells in his hands. By their sickly-green color, she suspected neither she nor Caleb would like the effect they produced.

Behind by several paces stood a petite woman with large, doe-like eyes.

Anna.

Lilliana's gaze zeroed in on her cousin, who set her left hand on a cocked hip. A large stone winked fire from the third finger on her left hand, and the same glittering hardness played across her features.

Betrayal lanced through Lilliana. Tío Manny hadn't sold his daughter off to the Underground as she suspected. Her cousin might as well have punched her in the gut with the hand that wore the engagement ring.

Derwin *tsked.* "Get up Lilliana. It's unseemly the way you recline on the floor."

She wished she had more bullets for Caleb's gun. Spelled rounds would wipe the sneer off both Derwin's and Anna's faces. All she had was her shifter's knife.

Caleb's knife.

Slowly, she rose to her feet, using his large body as a screen for slipping into the purse at her waist. Knife in hand, she bumped into him, hopefully appearing unsteady on her feet.

She used the distraction technique to slide the knife into the small of Caleb's back at his waistband.

Without even looking in her direction, he reached for his pants.

"Stop, or you'll wish I killed you quick." The mage's tone carried a hint of worry. Good. The jerk would be more likely to be distracted.

Caleb held up his hands. Neither the garment nor the knife would stay in place for long. "You can either let me hold up my pants, or your girl there gets to see why once you go shifter, you never go back."

Her cousin's eyes widened, then speculation turned her features coy.

Lilliana snorted a laugh and slid a snide side-eye to her ex. "Anna might not want to see that. No potion she could create would make you compare..."

"For God's sake—hold your pants up." Derwin's voice held a high but furious edge.

Lilliana barely suppressed a second burst of laughter. Derwin's lovemaking had bored her beyond tears. If Caleb's manhood even remotely matched his physical size, the mage indeed had something to be insecure about. Regardless, hopefully the shifter got the hint that Anna wasn't as much a threat as Derwin.

"Give me the amulet and the thumb drive." His words were tight with anger, possibly knowing her thoughts. The glow in the spell balls grew brighter, and he narrowed his eyes at Caleb. "Or I'll make sure Rover here dies a painful death."

That he took his focus off her said all she needed to know. He didn't think she was a threat at all. Yeah, she was a Level One mage, but she'd never been good at the mechanics of magical battle.

Didn't matter. She had a shifter on her side.

11

THESE UNDERGROUND GUYS were dumber than rocks. Derwin must not figure Lilliana would cause him any trouble.

Caleb could capitalize on the mage's mistake. Though Sedona Vortex wasn't heavily staffed, there was a small security garrison. Hopefully, someone monitored this interaction on a camera. Someone who wasn't also a paid Underground informant.

Lilliana slipped a chain from over her head. A charm dangled at the end. "You mean this amulet?"

The man held out his hand, now empty of the swirling, ugly green spell. Anticipation hung in Caleb's chest. If the mage would just take his focus from him for one moment...

Derwin said with a mean tone, "Yes, *that* amulet, the one you stole from your uncle. *And* the thumb drive."

After digging in the purse at her waist, she withdrew a small, metallic rectangle. "This thumb drive?"

"Goddammit. Yes. Now bring them to me." He took a step back. "But don't try anything, or—"

"Yeah, I know, or Rover gets it." Her deadpan delivery suggested an eye roll, but Caleb remained focused on Derwin, ready to spring at the right moment.

The mage's features tightened. "You always were a pain in the ass. I told Manny we should just take you from Santiago's, but he didn't want his hands dirty. He thought you'd come to us, like in Elgin and tonight. You would've fetched a pretty price at the auction. And now I'm out my commission."

Rage seared through Caleb. Even if she handed over what Stanford wanted, probability said he'd still try to take Lilliana again and eliminate Caleb. He doubled his determination to save her once more.

The gloating mage's taunts didn't seem to bother Lilliana. "When Grandmother hears how you used to say she was old and how you could replace her, maybe she'll stop carping on me for dumping you."

Ouch. Caleb snickered.

Derwin's face popped red, and he opened his mouth several times, but nothing came out. Moments later, his features gained a purple cast and seemed to swell with his fury, rather like the girl who turned into a blueberry in the candy factory.

Despite his tight-lipped scowl, Derwin maintained a laser focus on Caleb, then he said, "Bring me the damn amulet and the drive."

Caleb waited for his moment. If the mage changed his attention one iota, he and Lilliana had a chance. If not, he'd have to make his own opening. His muscles bunched. Losing Lilliana was not an option.

She crossed the twenty or so feet, her hand holding the items outstretched.

When she came close enough, Derwin lunged toward her hand.

The amulet and drive fell toward the floor, and Derwin's gaze darted to his prizes.

Caleb reached for his knife, drew the deadly length of fae silver, and hurled the blade. Bullseye, buried to the hilt in the center of the mage's chest. Lucky for Caleb, his predator's enhanced reaction time beat the mage's.

At the same moment his blade impacted, Lilliana's spells landed, one on Derwin and the other on Anna.

Rather than slinging the glowing green ball that remained in his palm, the mage fell face forward to the floor with a *crack* when his forehead hit the granite. Anna landed similarly, minus the knife, but a small dark ball rolled from the witch's palm and across the floor, stopping inches from Caleb's foot. He bent to pick up whatever the witch had dropped.

"Don't touch it."

Lilliana's tone held a sharp immediacy, and he drew back his hand.

She crossed to him and knelt to examine the round object, about the size of a golf ball, black with red and sparkling copper streaks. A sound almost like a growl came from her, then she stood with a grimace on her features. "I think that's a nuclear heart charm."

He took an involuntary step back. One sure way to kill someone from Clan Shifter or Sanguis? Incinerate the heart. Looked like Caleb bet right, except Anna, rather than Stanford, would've tried to kill him. He rubbed his chest. "Thanks. That could've hurt."

She huffed a laugh devoid of amusement and stared at her cousin who remained sprawled on the floor. "You're welcome. I had no idea she taken up her craft's illegal side."

"That may be why she was with Derwin. I bet he asked you to do similar things, but you resisted."

"Not asked per se. Merely suggested that death and other illegal spells were a very lucrative trade. Multiple times. With a hopeful expression." A fierce frown tugged at her brows. "It was mostly the reason I broke up with him."

"Glad you did. What was the other reason?" With her comments earlier, perhaps he didn't satisfy her—emotionally *or* physically.

She opened her mouth to speak, then closed her lips and glanced down to the charm. "I nuh-need t-to get th-that." Lilliana shuddered, then she clasped her hands together hard until they were bloodless.

Oh boy. The events of the last several minutes had come home to roost. The last thing she needed to do was try to contain the deadly magical charm.

He pulled her into his embrace, and she didn't resist. Shivers wracked her body, and she wrapped her arms around him tight enough he might think her a boa constrictor shifter if he didn't know better. "Shh. I've got you. It's just a little adrenaline dumping into your system."

Lilliana nodded her head, which she'd tucked into his chest.

While he wanted to revel in the fact he held her, the two prone magic wielders must remain his focus. "How long before Anna wakes up?"

"The portal drained most of my magic, so about ten minutes," she mumbled. Then her gaze rose to his. Her eyes were wide with wonder. "How'd you know where to find me?"

"I got a call from Cheese. She said you would be at the Underground auction and that your name was being circulated as a last-minute addition." His jaw tightened. "I just missed you at the vortex since I had to go standby. Luckily, Brie got me entrance to the auction. Apparently, my family name is still good for something, but I have no idea how she managed it all that fast."

"She's good, that's for sure." She scrunched her face. "I'm sorry for zapping you at her cabin. Sometimes my spells go haywire if I'm nervous. Lord knows I can't hit the broadside of Enchanted Rock when I throw. So maybe Derwin and Anna will wake up before I think."

He silently cursed. Because he was unwilling to let her go, he'd use the hand still holding up his pants to retrieve the phone in his front pocket. "I'm going to call this in."

Before he let go of his waistband, a male voice said, "Freeze. NAC Security."

Caleb did as instructed, but he prepared to defend Lilliana just in case this person was a threat.

A tall, dark-haired male strode into the wide hallway from the main corridor with five other individuals, all wearing the black uniform of North American Council Security. The officers arrayed to either side of him. "NACS Officer Espina. Step away from each other and show your hands."

Lilliana raised her gaze to his, trust shining bright. She'd follow his lead.

Though he'd never met Espina, Caleb had heard of him and how he'd helped save the Clan Magic chairman's wife. Definitely not a sorcerer to trifle with. Not to mention, Caleb had no idea of the other security officers' clan affiliations.

However much it hurt to let Lilliana go and raise his hands, Caleb did as ordered, all while his wolf howled at the separation.

"Who are you?" Espina's gaze went back and forth between them both.

He was proud of her strong voice when she answered, "Lilliana Vargas, mage."

"Caleb Coffey, shifter. I work for Nathan Hebert."

The officer raised his chin a fraction, a subtle indicator he recognized Caleb's boss, though the name wasn't a "get out of jail free" card.

"Be careful." Lilliana kept her hands in the air and nodded to the ground near Caleb's feet. "There's a Nuclear Heart charm right there."

Espina's gaze flashed to hers, the furrow between his brows even deeper. "Yours?"

"No. My cousin, Anna Santiago—right there." She canted her head to indicate the unconscious woman. "That's Derwin Stanford, mage."

"I know Stanford." The officer's tone indicated he cared little for Derwin, but then his eyes widened, only to narrow into slits. "Who hit him with the knife?"

"He did, officer. He killed Derwin." Anna's groggy voice came along with her arm limply pointing at Caleb.

His muscles tightened, but he knew better than to respond.

"No." Lilliana's voice had risen to near panic. "I mean he threw the knife—"

"I think we need to have our rights read and attorney present, Officer Espina." Caleb shot her a glance from the corner of his eye, and his tone brooked no argument. Lilliana had been working with Clan Magic Security, at least she believed. Best to give her some time to collect her thoughts and someone to advocate for her if needed.

The officer's shoulders stiffened. "Ms. Vargas?"

Lilliana ducked her head, almost as if a submissive wolf, very unlike the woman Caleb knew. With a breathy voice, she said, "Yes, I think I'd like to have my attorney present."

The slash of Espina's lips indicated his displeasure. "Very

well. Take these three into custody. And call the medics for Derwin Stanford. I'd like him alive."

12

"But you're family," Anna whispered urgently. She turned down the corners of her mouth and her glare turned vicious. "You can say I was forced to make the charm."

Lilliana leaned back against the chair she'd been directed to sit in by one of the NACS officers. During transport, she hadn't been able to talk to her cousin, nor had she been able to demand an apology for leading Lilliana on a wild sprite chase that almost got her killed.

Then there was the itty-bitty fact that Anna had made the Nuclear Heart charm and probably would've killed Caleb. So Lilliana stewed and stewed until she and her cousin were deposited in this row of chairs.

One after the other, she and Anna had been allowed to contact an attorney. Lilliana dreaded the call to her grandmother. Right after the clipped, "I'll be there in forty minutes," the line went dead. Now, the two officers standing guard were off a short distance, and Anna took the opportunity to start in that she couldn't go to jail, how it would embarrass the family.

Grr. Lilliana wanted to jump up and choke her cousin who sat four chairs from her. Why had she ever bought into Anna's penchant to play the victim? With the spelled bindings holding her arms behind her, Lilliana couldn't even leap up and smack some sense into the witch. Well, she could probably ditch the Santiago-produced cuffs, but it might freak out the officers, and she didn't need that right now.

In fact, what she needed was a cousin who owned up to her own actions.

"Dammit, Lilliana," Anna hissed. "It's not like Grandmother won't get you out of any trouble. She won't help me because I'm a mutt."

Lilliana wanted to roll her eyes, but she knew her cousin was right. Though usually the attention came in the form of "helpful" comments that stung worse than a scorpion, Grandmother had always favored Lilliana, a mage. She kept her voice low when she said, "You didn't have to possess the charm, Anna. That's all I saw."

Anna flopped back in her chair and said in an ugly tone, "You're such a bitch. Derwin was right about you."

At this point, Lilliana couldn't give two gnome shits for what Derwin thought of her. What was going on with Caleb? He was the one who threw the knife and probably saved her life. Derwin would recover, surely.

What she couldn't understand was the need for an attorney. Neither she nor Caleb had done anything wrong. She leaned her head back against the wall and reflected on the last couple of weeks. Maybe a lawyer *was* the better route. But dealing with her grandmother atop the wild day made her want to melt into the cracks in Enchanted Rock's pink granite floor.

One of the guards ambled over and made her get up. Was she going to jail? He stopped at an open door to a room and relief sluiced through her. Once he removed her cuffs, he pointed to the seat she could occupy.

She slumped in the uncomfortable plastic chair at a table with a chipped, faux-wood top. Besides the other three identical chairs, the only other item of interest in the room was a large mirror on the wall facing her. She didn't need to be a rocket scientist to know someone could be watching.

While she sat at the table for what had to be the better part of an hour, the events of the day—hell, the events since Detective Slocomb contacted her—went over and over in her mind. She had no doubt that Caleb had done the right thing by throwing the knife. Her spell could've gone wonky, and Derwin could've killed both him and her. If only her shifter hadn't been swept up in this.

The door flew open, and Carolina Vargas glided into the room.

Lilliana's grandmother had dressed in a smart suit and heels and gilded herself with full makeup. Not a hair dared to stray out of place from the sleek fall of her steel-gray, bobbed hair. She'd been a North American Council judge for many years, and even after retirement, remained a sought-after, ludicrously expensive defense attorney. With a pointed look at Lilliana, she dropped her leather briefcase onto the table with a solid thunk. She glanced at the mirror, then wiggled her manicured fingers, casting a silencing spell like Lilliana had used earlier with Caleb at the mansion.

For a moment, Lilliana wanted to shrink away from her grandmother's glare because she'd disappointed her family once more. Then the word "no" came into her thoughts. She'd done nothing wrong. No. She would not be berated like the five-year-old who'd prematurely dipped her fingers into the icing of her own beautifully decorated birthday cake.

No. She would not be scolded like the eight-year-old girl who'd gotten dirt on her party dress.

No. She would not be lectured like when she said she wasn't sure if she loved Derwin.

No.

The word repeated over and over and over, Lilliana's spine growing stiffer with each recitation.

"Well, what do you have to say for yourself?" Her grandmother crossed her arms and tapped an impatient toe.

Lilliana settled a sweetly sarcastic smile on her lips. "It's been a rough day, but I'm fine thanks. How are you?"

Her grandmother's eyes narrowed, probably with the saccharine tone Lilliana had used. But the matriarch had been a judge for too long to easily cede the upper hand. "Don't play games with me. What happened?"

Her tone had softened enough to lose the diamond-hard edge, and Lilliana took the shift as a small win. She provided the details, from the time she'd spoken with the Clan Magic detective over two weeks ago to the present. She didn't think Grandmother cared to hear Anna's opinion or excuses, since she'd barely tolerated that particular granddaughter since her birth.

During the story, the older woman had taken a seat, removed a paper pad and pen from her case, then began taking notes. When Lilliana finished speaking, the older woman glanced up from writing, her lids narrowed, gaze razor sharp. "So you did nothing wrong?"

"Not to hurt anyone. Permanently, that is. I mean, the Underground people might be a little unhappy I shot them with the spelled bullets..."

Her grandmother waived her hand in a dismissive way. "Who was this shifter you mentioned? This Caleb."

For a moment Lilliana paused, unwilling to expose him to her grandmother's scorn. "Caleb Coffey."

"Coffey. Coffey." The older woman tapped the tip of her index finger against her lips. "Tall? Red hair? Hazel eyes? Wolf?"

"Yes." All of that but so much more. "Tough" and "skilled" could be added to his descriptor list. He didn't have to come after her when she'd made her stupid decision to go to the Underground auction. Nor did he have to kiss her like she was the only one for him. "Special" could be added too. "Gorgeous," with all those yummy muscles...

Her grandmother snapped her fingers in front of Lilliana's face and brought her back to the interrogation room's cold reality. Didn't matter how special or attractive she thought Caleb. She had a job to do.

Tell the truth.

The door opened, and Officer Espina poked his head into the room. "You ready, counselor?"

With a regal nod befitting a fae queen, Grandmother said, "Yes." To Lilliana, she whispered harshly, "Wait for my nod before answering any questions."

Lilliana could only jerk her chin in acknowledgement since Espina and another officer with a notepad entered, then both sat at the table.

Once the other officer settled, Espina said, "Why don't you tell me what happened in the corridor."

"What are the charges she faces?" Her grandmother's sentence sizzled between his question and Lilliana's answer.

"Nothing." He favored her with a curl to his lips that lacked humor. "At least right now."

"Then she has nothing to say, and we'll be leaving."

"What?" The word burst from Lilliana. She'd always been truthful, and that fact wouldn't end tonight.

Her grandmother grabbed Lilliana's hand and squeezed hard. The older woman said in a harsh tone that could've cut fae fyre crystal, "Listen to me, girl."

Lilliana snatched her fingers from her grandmother's grasp. Caleb wasn't responsible for any of this. Of anyone, she'd made this mess by panicking about her cousin and acting on the behalf of someone in magical law enforcement. Not Lilliana's fault at all. "I am absolutely telling what happened tonight, as well as about two weeks back."

"One moment please." Grandmother didn't wait for the officer's approval and created the silencing spell once more. With a fierce glower, she said, "You will listen to me. I know what's best for you and the family. You will—"

"Like you knew what was best when you ordered me to marry Derwin?" Fury hotter than the sun burned within Lilliana. She deserved to make her own choices, family be damned.

For a moment Grandmother sat with her jaw hanging, as if she couldn't believe Lilliana had the temerity to cut her off. Rarely did someone find Carolina Vargas at a loss for words. Lilliana took the advantage. "Like he was acceptable when Derwin, despite the fact he's part of the Underground and kidnaps and sells paranormals—like he wanted to do to me, mind you— for profit?"

Grandmother's mouth opened, then shut, then she said, "I'm sure that's just a misunderstanding—"

"Like when Derwin called you old and told me on multiple occasions that he would do a better job of running the family?"

"He said what?" The older woman's angry tone suggest Lilliana had touched the older woman's last nerve.

"Glad that finally got your attention, because you obviously don't care about me, only the family name." Lilliana dissolved the muting spell and turned to Officer Espina with a newfound sense of purpose guiding her. "Seems I don't need an attorney after all. Counselor Vargas has decided it might be better to represent her other granddaughter, Anna Santiago." She shot her grandmother a hard stare, daring her to continue the argument in the open. "Wish Anna well for me, please."

Hot red spots of color flagged the older woman's cheeks, but she didn't contradict Lilliana. Instead, she rose to her full height, gathered her briefcase, and glided from the room without a backward glance.

Lilliana wove her fingers together and rested them on the worn tabletop. "Now, officers, should I start from the beginning?"

13

CALEB SAT in his SUV surveilling the dark parking lot of Lilliana's apartment complex. During the early morning hours, little stirred. A couple of people had recently left in their vehicles, presumably for work, but all else remained quiet throughout the modest but scrupulously clean development. The lack of activity suggested law abiding residents and a location safer than many. Good.

He'd backed into a spot almost across from her assigned space, which had been empty since he arrived about an hour and a half ago. He'd doubted someone would've driven her home. Since the complex sat at least forty miles from Enchanted Rock, she would've had to portal a couple of times without using a car. After the crap day she had, he doubted she had the reserves.

What if she went to stay with a family member instead of coming back here? With her lineage, her family most likely lived in Illusion, the hidden city where many of Clan Magic chose to dwell. If she were tired, she might've stopped there. He didn't have an amulet to grant him access to the guarded city, so charging into the Vargas mansion was out. Meeting her here made more sense. His wolf paced in the back of his mind.

Need, his feral side whined.

Yeah, buddy, I get it. I like her too.

Now.

Not helping me focus. Go lay down.

In a huff, the wolf settled, but the presence stayed in Caleb's mind, much like the desire to ensure Lilliana was okay. While he'd said he wanted an attorney, he'd never intended on using a lawyer's services. He needed time to settle and think about all that happened. Adrenaline had a way of making you forget events, only for them to pop into your head hours later. And with all the adrenaline the evening produced, both he and Lilliana would need as many faculties as possible.

He'd declined the lawyer when offered the telephone, accepted a cup of what turned out to be horrible coffee, then settled in to tell Espina everything he knew, from the time he first encountered Lilliana in Elgin to the moment NACS showed up in the Sedona Vortex hallway. He did keep out the kissing and how hard Lilliana made him and the fact he believed she was his mate.

No reason for them to know *that* much.

In the end, Espina told Caleb he wouldn't be charged with a crime. Further, Caleb learned NACS had a mole inside the organization, and that Derwin had drawn Manny Santiago into business with the Underground. Apparently, Derwin would live, though Caleb wasn't sure how to feel about the mage's survival. On one hand, death seemed reasonable for the harm he caused. On the other, the mage faced charges that would probably land him in prison for a couple of hundred years, hopefully long enough to ensure he died behind bars.

Tough choice, until Caleb considered the bastard probably treated Lilliana abominably. Definitely the first option.

Not that he had the deciding capability. Well, he might've earlier if he'd separated the mage's head from the rest of his body. No coming back from that. But no. His damn need for justice wouldn't allow him to kill a defenseless being. He'd downed Stanford, and Lilliana doubled up with an immobility spell a fraction of a second later. Threat mitigated and no need for deadly force.

His wolf growled in the back of his mind.

Bah. Damn internal compass.

Caleb shifted in his seat and resolved himself for long hours of surveillance. He scanned the eastern horizon, where the barest hit of dawn began to fringe the night sky. At this time of year, the clock must read around five.

Headlights swept the cars when a compact sedan pulled slowly into the lot. He sat straighter when he noticed it was the same make and model as the one noted in the report Cheese ran today—no, now yesterday. Both he and his wolf sat up straight. When the vehicle pulled into Lilliana's assigned spot, he got out but remained next to his SUV. Surprising a paranormal at close range in a parking lot during the early morning hours was rarely a good idea unless you intended to nab them.

The door to her sedan opened slowly and remained so for several moments. No overhead dome light appeared, and his view was obscured by the headrest. What was she doing? He began to cross to her, but she then unfolded herself from the driver's seat. He halted. Her shoulders sagged, and her back bowed as if broken. What had they done to her?

He cleared his throat.

Lilliana startled, then whirled, already prepared to sling spells. At least she had some fight left in her.

He held his hands palm out at chest height and scanned her pinched features. "Just me. Wanted to make sure you got home okay."

Lilliana swayed, then slumped against her car.

He raced over and caught her before she slid to the ground.

"So tired." Her voice was a bit garbled.

She seemed so light in his arms, and his anger at Stanford and her family grew. Instead of growling at her like his wolf wanted, he said gently, "Let's get you inside."

Like a puppeteer controlled the jerky movement, she merely nodded her head.

He knew her apartment to be on the third floor, and he guided her up the stairs.

Despite her exhaustion, he didn't have to carry her, and he was impressed by the sheer will she exhibited. But when she fumbled with her key, he gently removed the ring from her fingers, unlocked the deadbolt, and opened the door.

She entered and practically dragged her feet halfway through what appeared to be her sparsely decorated living room from what he could view from his position at the threshold. A club chair sat at right angles to a small sectional. A sleek coffee table sporting only coasters sat in the middle of the seating group. On a side table, a lamp. Nothing on the walls. No knickknacks. She stopped, then pivoted toward him, a tired twist to her lips. "You coming in?"

Three words had never sounded so good. "I didn't want to presume."

Her back seemed to straighten a bit and a tired, but sweet, smile crossed her face. "Though we've known each other for—what?—three days, I don't know why, but I trust you."

His wolf howled in approval. "Longer. Remember last month when you hit me with the spell?"

Caleb shut the door behind him, all the while pinning her with his stare. Her eyes seemed huge in her face, with dark crescents underneath, but she didn't waver when he came to her. Without realizing he'd moved them, he'd placed his hands on the soft skin of her biceps and he swept his thumbs in a soothing motion.

"Sorry for hurting you," she mumbled.

"I don't think you really meant to." Ever so slowly, he and she came together until his hips and thighs mingled with hers.

"My spells go wonky if I'm nervous." She licked her lip, snagging the lower between her teeth. Her gazed dropped to his mouth, and his heart leapt. Then her stomach growled audibly, and her cheeks reddened in the most charming manner.

He fit his forehead against hers. "Probably a good thing."

"Why?" she whispered.

"Because I have a feeling I'm not going to want to stop once we start. Assuming you're okay with me finding every secret spot that makes you scream with pleasure."

The blush grew brighter, but a hint of defiance wiped away the embarrassment. "If I wasn't so damned hungry and tired, I'd take you up on that offer."

His stomach rolled a bit in sympathy with hers. It had been hours since he hadn't eaten his dinner at the steakhouse. "Hungry first?"

"I've got some meals in the freezer. Not much in the way of meat." Her gaze darted to the kitchen he'd passed on his way into the apartment.

The growl emanating from his abdomen protested the concept. "No microwave stuff. Too tiny. Too tasteless. You have any eggs?"

"I got a dozen last week but haven't touched them yet."

"I'll scavenge, and you can take a load off on the couch."

With reluctance, he released her arms and stepped back. His wolf immediately whined, but food also sounded good, so he settled, waiting.

She shook her head in the negative. "The couch is too comfortable. I'll conk out."

"You could nap for a bit." His body came to attention with the idea sexy times might be back on the menu if she rested while he cooked.

"I'll be too gone and won't want to eat. It's been days since I've gotten a good night's sleep."

"I'll try to keep you up then." He moved past the small dining table, around the peninsula, and to the kitchen's refrigerator. A scan of the interior revealed a carton of milk, a dozen eggs, a partial bag of fresh broccoli florets, half a pint of cherry tomatoes, half of an onion, and some luncheon meat. In the freezer, he found a partial bag of frozen hashbrowns. He'd seen bachelor pads with more food. In the condiments stored on the door, he pulled a container of parmesan cheese. If the expiration dates and his sense of smell were to be trusted on the milk and the sliced, smoked chicken packet, they were both edible.

Frittata.

He glanced across the counter to where she'd propped herself on a barstool. "Bowl for a dozen eggs?"

"I'll get it." She moved into the kitchen and squeezed behind him, her front brushing against his ass.

He sucked in a breath since he'd barely been keeping his arousal at bay.

From a cabinet in the far corner, she pulled a large, clear mixing bowl and set it in front of him. A soft smile canted her lips in a direction which said sleepy-sexy. "Anything else?"

"Absolutely." He locked gazes with her and allowed all his dirty thoughts to light a fire in his eyes.

Her mouth parted, and she licked her lips.

How he wished he could lose himself in her right now, but nourishment came first. "I need...a large skillet."

"Sure," she said with a dry chuckle. She bent to a lower a cabinet in front of her, slowly, deliberately, and his focus couldn't have left her ass even if his eyes had been cut from his head. She rummaged, her butt wiggling in the most attractive way, then brought out a cast-iron skillet and put it next to the bowl. "Anything else?"

"I'm good. For now." How he managed to say the strangled words with how his tongue cleaved to the roof of his mouth was beyond him. *Nourishment first, moron.*

He set the oven for the appropriate temperature, prepped the skillet, then put it on the burner to warm. He used a cutting board and knife from a block on the counter to chop the onion. Once he'd dumped the aromatics and the potato shreds into the hot pan to brown, he turned back and found she'd moved to a barstool on the other side of the peninsula and propped her chin in her palm. He broke the silence. "What took you so long? I got here two hours before you did."

She watched him crack a couple of eggs then said, "I had to have a discussion with my grandmother and parents afterward."

Oh boy. He finished cracking the last egg. If his experience was anything like hers, the meeting couldn't have gone well. "Nothing like family drama to take you from tired to exhausted."

Her huff could've been interpreted as amusement or frustration or possibly both. "Ain't that the truth. Especially when it's something they don't want to hear."

"What didn't they want to hear?" He poured the milk and began to whisk.

"About my uncle, Anna, and Derwin." She crossed her arms and leaned her elbows on the countertop. "What they'd been doing and how it was going to blow back against the family."

Ugh. "How did they take it?" After adding a dash of salt and pepper, he turned to the stove and poured the egg mixture into the pan, pivoted back, then set to cutting strips of the lunch meat.

"Not well, since my family puts public perception and archaic duty above all else."

He laid in the meat, spread a couple handfuls of the broccoli, then scattered the small tomatoes with fair evenness. On top of that, he added a couple of hefty handfuls of flaked parmesan. While the bottom of the frittata cooked, he turned back to her, leaning his butt against the counter and propping his hands behind him on the granite. "Tell me about archaic. My family has been trying to set me up with other shifter females from the right kind of family for years."

"You too?" She slumped against her barstool. "Grandmother tried to tell me that the whole debacle was due to the fact her daughter married a witch instead of the mage she was supposed to."

"Sounds like something my dad would say."

"Good grief. There's more than one of these people? Gah. I mentioned to her that she wanted me to marry a mage who was neck-deep in the Underground and working shoulder to shoulder with her son-in-law." Lilliana rolled her eyes. "She didn't acknowledge my point and changed topics like any good lawyer."

The woman sounded like a winner. His sympathy for his mate grew while his wolf wanted to howl at the probability her family—and ultimately Lilliana—wouldn't accept him. He forced a casual note into his voice when he said, "That's a lot from your grandmother. What did your parents think?"

"Exactly what Grandmother told them to think. Mom suggested not all sorcerers and witches were bad, but Grandmother put her right back in line. It's pathetic, really. I mean, what if..." Lilliana dropped her gaze and began to trace a pattern on the counter with her finger. Her teeth worried at her bottom lip.

Could she... After several minutes of silence, instinct instructed him to give her a push. "What if what?"

She pulled her hand into her lap and sat straighter in her seat. Finally, she lifted her gaze to his. The solemn expression on her features stilled him and his breath hung in his chest.

"What if I decided I wanted to date a shifter?"

14

LILLIANA HELD her breath and forced herself to keep eye contact with Caleb. The only sound in her apartment was the gentle burble from the eggs in the skillet.

He'd been still and silent for far too long. Had she gauged the situation incorrectly? She chickened out and dropped her gaze to the frittata next to him on the stove. "I mean, maybe dating was the wrong word. Maybe you're just looking for fun times."

Good grief, was she babbling again? She shut her mouth and resisted the urge to bang her forehead on the counter for being such an idiot.

Still he said nothing, but he did unfold his arms, turned to the skillet, and lifted it by the silicone handle she'd placed on earlier. Worry built within her with every second he remained mute. Once he put the food into the oven, he set the timer for fifteen minutes.

She had a full-blown apartment block worth of tension on

her shoulders by the time he came around the kitchen peninsula and stopped before her. His features were grave, not mad, but as if what he would say or do carried the import of the world.

Then a grin grew on his lips, and his irises turned to bright copper. “I absolutely want to date you, Lilliana Vargas.”

Sprites seemed to knock around in her stomach. “Are you sure? I mean, I’m not tall and gorgeous like most of the shifter women you’re used to.” Who in the hell had taken over her brain? Was she trying to talk him out of it? Or was she fishing for compliments? She hung her head and covered her eyes with one hand. “You don’t have to answer that.”

“Why *wouldn’t* I want to date you? You’re beautiful and smart and you believe in family, or you wouldn’t have tried to help your cousin. Plus, you’re a helluva kisser.”

When she snapped her head up, she met his hungry gaze. Then her focus slipped to his mouth, and suddenly she was short of breath. “Really?”

“Really. Especially the kissing part.”

She stretched out and threaded her fingers into his thick, wavy, surprisingly silky hair. He offered no resistance when she tugged him forward to meet her lips.

Before, he had taken the initiative, but now she felt emboldened and, for the first time in her life, sexy. Her lids descended and she continued, guided by pure sensation.

She fit her mouth to his supple lips, then swept her tongue in a request for entry. With a groan, he let her inside. Her mouth slid against his, time after time, stoking the fire in her core, making her breasts heavy with need for his fingers and his lips on the peaked points that already ached for his touch.

She fanned one of her hands down his chest over the T-shirt he wore tucked into his jeans. His breathing hitched when she slid over his nipple, and a part of her brain catalogued the reaction for later. Impatient to touch his skin, she pulled the cotton from his waistband and skimmed her fingers along his ribs, then around to the small of his back.

Yum. Tight, toned, and tempting.

More. She scooted forward on the barstool, then split her legs and pulled him into the "V" she'd created. When he pressed his hips against her, his hard cock made her moan.

He pulled his lips from hers and trailed feathery kisses to her ear. "See how you affect me?"

The warm breath from his murmur tickled her ear, then he nipped her earlobe and she nearly dissolved with want. When his lips forged a path of fire down her neck, she tipped her head back, helpless to do anything other than rock against his length.

Another groan came from him, this one more gloriously rough and needy. With a mock growl in his voice he said, "Woman, you are going to pay for that."

"Promise?" Her tone carried a raspy sexiness, one she'd never heard before. How had this man made her feel more like a siren than anyone else?

"I promise you will pay dearly. Over and over." His warm breath caressed the skin of her collarbone, and he tunneled his hand under her lace blouse, splaying across her torso, coming dangerously close to her breast.

She gasped and pushed her chest forward, desperate for him to touch her there. "I heard someone recently say that once you go shifter you never go back."

He chuckled. While one palm teased her by stroking around her breast, he flicked open a button on her blouse with his other hand. His gaze met hers, his irises lit with copper flame. "You will never go back. That I do promise."

When he cupped her breast with his hot palm, she lost all

rational thought. Framing his face with her hands, she brought his lips back to hers and kissed him with every ounce of her passion. In return, he stroked and kneaded her over her bra. She needed to get the undergarment off. Now.

Like he'd read her mind, he snapped the thin strip of fabric holding the cups together. He slipped free another blouse button, then another. He bent, and his hot mouth enveloped her nipple, and she thought she'd come right then with the way he swamped her senses.

"Yessss..."

With one hand she cradled his head against her, urging him without words to spend time there and do—oh god—*that*. Nipping at the bud, pulling, laving, sucking. First one, then the other and back again.

Restless desperation rocketed through her veins. She needed to get closer to him, no fabric, just skin to skin. She pulled up his shirt, spread her hands against his chest, found one nipple and scratched lightly with her fingernail. He paused for the barest second, then huffed a gentle laugh and returned with a vengeance to her breasts. Then suddenly, he stopped.

What? Over the pounding of her pulse, she dimly heard a beeping.

The timer.

Noooooo.

"Be right back." She might've chuckled at the frustration in his short phrase, but it matched her own.

When he moved away, she shivered with the loss of his heat. Reason said better him take out the food than the scent of burnt eggs stinking up the apartment.

Gah. She hated reason sometimes.

Impatient to touch him once more, she left the stool. She

had a smoking hot man in her apartment, and she wanted him this minute. Food be damned.

He'd put the skillet on a trivet next to the oven and before he could turn, she put her arms around his waist and laid her cheek against his back. With her hands, she roamed over his tight abs, teased him by brushing against the edge of his jeans. His heavy heartbeats and shallow, swift breathing gratified her —he was as needy as she.

For a moment, she gloried in the mere connection. Then she felt his muscles tense, and she ceased her caresses. Before she could ask what was wrong, he said, "I have something I need to tell you."

An awful suspicion crossed her mind, and she removed her fingers from the hard planes under his waistband. "You have a mate."

"Well, yes, I do, but it's not what you think."

She released him and swung away toward the living room. Tears brimmed her eyes, and a searing fury lit her heart. She straightened her blouse and yanked the open sides together, though her shaking fingers couldn't pull the buttons through the slits. Just her fucking luck. "You have a mate. Of course you do. Geezus."

He rushed around the peninsula. "Wait, Lilliana. It's you. You're my mate."

Surely she hadn't heard him correctly? She pivoted to face him, her heart thundering in her chest.

For a moment, silence reigned, then his lopsided smile faltered. "I didn't want you to feel obligated, but I didn't want you to think I wasn't honest with you."

She stared into his eyes, taking Caleb in as if for the first time. The proud clan had a major weakness, and the implication hit her hard. "Wolves mate for life."

"I know. But you're under no obligation. We should date first, then see if it works out for you." His stillness said her next words held his future in her hands.

"But aren't there consequences for you if I don't, if we don't..."

"Some." He stepped forward until his hands bracketed her shoulders. His thumbs brushed against her skin, soft and soothing. "But this isn't about me. This is about you. Getting time to know me. No strings attached."

That he would consider her walking away if she wanted was enough for her to know he would be worth the effort. So unlike her family.

She took the step that brought her against him, then wrapped her arms around his waist. He stilled, and she laid her head against his chest so she could hear his heart beat, while her body reveled in the connection.

Mine.

He hadn't drawn a breath in several moments. Hell. She lifted her gaze and found him watching her intently, waiting for her answer. Perhaps he read something of her decision in her features because he cupped her hips with his hands, and she could've melted with his possessive touch. Instead, she trailed a finger down his chest. "I've heard that once you go shifter, you never go back."

The slowest, sexiest grin crossed his features, and his eyes lit copper flame. Then doubt doused the fires. "You sure you—"

She silenced his question with two fingers over his mouth. "I want you to show me why."

With a sharp inhale, he dropped his lids, desire smoldering behind them. "My pleasure."

When he swept her up into his arms, she chuckled. "But the frittata."

"Food can wait." Delicious determination glowed bright in his gaze. "I have some convincing to do."

The End

Hello! Just a short message about a couple of important things.

First, I hope you enjoyed this novella and would like to ask if you could leave a review of *The Wolf's Mage*? We independently published authors need your input, as do other readers to find the stories they want to read. It can be as simple or as detailed as you like. Thank you in advance!

Second, be sure to check out my website for more stories in the Enchanted Rock Immortals World. There you can also find my **FREE Enchanted Rock Immortals ebook**, *A Puma's Second Chance*. I have other freebies I release exclusively to newsletter subscribers, as well as a whole psychic cozy mystery series, *The Flannigan Sisters Psychic Mysteries*. All that and more are available at amandareidauthor.com!

Thank you so much, and until we read again,

Amanda

The Shifter's Sorcerer

An Enchanted Rock Immortals Novella

by Amanda Reid

Available Now in Kindle and Kindle Unlimited!

Hank and Thelma race to save their friends' wedding, but can they find their own happily ever after?

When her friend's wedding is sabotaged and the special day's dress lost, spell-challenged sorcerer Thelma Janson steps up with her boutique's magical dress designs. She hadn't counted on her assistance putting her in the crosshairs of a vengeful fae lord. Stepping up to keep her safe? "Mouse" the enigmatic, wildly attractive shifter who isn't at all interested in her...but makes her heart spark like she's been hit with a love charm.

Since the gorgeous Thelma has kept him at a distance, Hank "Mouse" Sullivan has tracked her from afar. If only it were as simple as stealing his heart with her offer to aid mutual friends despite the danger to herself and her business. Now, his protective wolf has claimed the vivacious sorcerer as his mate, a permanent attachment Hank could never break. Could this bright, compassionate woman who makes his wolf howl possibly consider crossing clans for a gargoyle-shifter hybrid?

The two may be able to help get the nuptials back on track, but can Hank save Thelma and their love, or will the fae lord's vengeance destroy any possibility of their future?

If your sweet spot is smack in the middle of Romantic Suspense and Urban Fantasy, you'll love Amanda's action-packed paranormal romances!

ABOUT THE AUTHOR

Amanda Reid authors not only Enchanted Rock Immortals urban fantasy romance novellas, but also the Flannigan Sisters Psychic Mysteries, a paranormal cozy mystery series.

Since she was young, she's been a lover of mystery, sci-fi, and paranormal genres. Amanda found her first romance book in her aunt's closet around thirteen years of age and quickly decided it needed to be added to her repertoire.

Beyond writing, Amanda was a career Army brat and lived in exotic locations like Tehran, Iran and DeRidder, Louisiana as a child. She dreamed of a career in the State Department, but ended up as a federal agent. For 24 years Amanda investigated murders, fraud, identity theft, drug trafficking and many other crimes before her retirement. As you can imagine, it's given her a wealth of inspiration for her mystery and urban fantasy stories.

She currently lives in Texas with her husband and two gonzo Australian Shepherds. Be sure to catch up with her on Facebook or Instagram. You can sign up to be notified about upcoming releases, free stories, and promos at her website—

amandareidauthor.com

Enchanted
Rock
Immortals

Made in the USA
Columbia, SC
12 November 2024

46295072R00076